December 22, 1958 - Randolph S. Coyner
" 28, " - Walter R. Firestone
January 4, 1959 - Patrica F. Chatham

THE PENTAGON CASE

A Novel of the Cold War

In war, morale is to materiel as three is to one.

—Napoleon

THE PENTAGON CASE

A Novel of the Cold War

by Victor J. Fox

FREEDOM PRESS · NEW YORK

FIRST EDITION

Library of Congress Catalog Card Number: 58-8546

MANUFACTURED IN THE U.S.A. BY THE COLONIAL PRESS INC.

This tale is for my wife, with all my love.

Contents

Foreword

The Pentagon Case is a work of fiction in the historical setting of the years between the Korean War and the launching of the first man-made earth satellites. It contains errors of fact. Historical dates, times, and places have been distorted or exaggerated in order to suit the story.

There is a Pentagon Building which actually exists, but in a form much different from the way it is described in this imaginary narrative, which is not a true story. No persons or situations like those described in this book exist or existed. None of its characters portrays any "real life" person whatsoever, either living or dead. The offices and titles of the imaginary characters do not exist: the Department of Defense itself has no Division of Special Investigations, Office of Public Relations, or Military Intelligence Division, nor does it have an Assistant Secretary for Military Morale, an Undersecretary for Industrial Mobilization, an Inspector General, a Surgeon General, or a Chaplain General. There is no Government Bureau of Security, Senate Committee for National Security, or Senate Committee on Pentagon Policy. The Federal Hospital referred to in the book is wholly imaginary and does not exist.

Ever since the first novel was written, readers have sought caricatures of living people in fiction, and no doubt there may be some readers of this book who will do the same. But those who do so will be disappointed: the fictitious backgrounds of the book's characters were contrived to motivate the story and do not portray either real persons or types of military or government officials. The Pentagon Building does have five sides, but it also has far more than the two entrances which are described in this book. It is also filled with dedicated Americans, both in mufti and in uniform, who have devoted their lives to their country's defense.

V. J. F.

CHAPTER ONE

Manpower Crisis

The Honorable J. Hardy Wells, Assistant Secretary of Defense for Military Morale, scanned the covering memorandum clipped to the top of a ten-page report on his desk, frowned slightly, and sat back in his chair to study the report itself. Half way through it, he shook his head in silent disapproval, pressed the starting button on the dictating machine on his desk, and addressed the microphone: "Memo for Colonel Howe: please send the analysis of Air Force resignations back to the Chief of Staff and tell him to classify it TOP SECRET. If those statistics ever hit the front pages, we'd all have Congress on our necks."

Secretary Wells dropped the report in the outgoing file, removed his shell-rimmed reading glasses, and rubbed his eyes. The papers in the outgoing file were stacked nearly a foot high, but the incoming file was piled even higher. He eyed it resentfully for a moment, sighed deeply, then stood up and stretched to straighten out his back muscles. On the wall behind his desk there was a large portrait of the nation's first Secretary of Defense, James V. Forrestal, between two draped American flags.

Wells glanced briefly at the portrait, then walked over to a window to rest his eyes. From the window he had an inspiring view which never failed to refresh him. Beyond the well-kept lawns lay the Pentagon's vast parking areas. Sunlight sparkled from the tops of thousands of bright-hued automobiles parked in neat rows like a display of the nation's industrial might. Across the broad Potomac River he could see the historic shrines of the nation's great leaders. To the left, classic in the simplicity of its lines, stood the Lincoln Memorial. To the right, among the cherry trees around the Tidal basin, gleamed the white marble dome of the Jefferson Memorial. At the far end of the oblong Reflecting Pool towered the lofty white shaft of the Washington Monument. Beyond and to the left he could see the White House, and upon the Hill, rising above the government office buildings that stretched in an unbroken line to the horizon, rose the dome of the Capitol.

Standing with his hands folded behind him, Hardy Wells surveyed this imposing view for several moments, then turned back to the pile of unfinished work on his desk. Like James Forrestal, Wells was a hard-working, conscientious citizen who had left a thriving business to serve his country. Wells kept approximately the same hours—from eight each morning until long after dark, seven days a week. Unlike Forrestal, who had become Secretary of Defense and had died in harness, Wells had already made up his mind that he would never accept an advancement beyond the level of Assistant Secretary, and that he would return to private life as soon as he could in all honesty consider his current responsibilities honorably discharged. He had accepted the assignment only after considerable urging from his close friend and college classmate Stacy Hale, who had been serving for the past year as Undersecretary of Defense for Industrial Mobilization.

At the age of forty, Wells was still slim and trim, well-groomed in the Ivy League tradition and fashionably gray at the temples. He held an honorary Colonelcy in the Air National Guard, having served in the U.S. Army Air Corps during World War II in aircraft procurement and briefly as a staff officer with the rank of Major. Shortly after the war, his father's sudden death had left him with a fortune which ran well into eight figures, plus the majority of the voting stock in one of the larger and more successful investment banking firms in the east. At forty he had been elevated to the presidency of his firm, which gave him enough leisure and more than enough income to qualify him for public service, had he aspired to political office. This he had studiously avoided, and had accepted the Pentagon assignment only because it was a non-political Presidential appointment. He was gratified, but not surprised, when his appointment was unanimously confirmed by the Senate after a routine review of his record.

Returning to his desk, Hardy Wells selected a bulky folder from the incoming file and glanced through the one-paragraph covering memorandum. Nodding approval, he signed it in the space indicated for his signature. The door to the adjoining office opened and his military aide, Colonel Matthew Howe, United States Air Force, entered the big room carrying a large file of papers.

The Secretary looked up inquiringly over the top of his reading glasses. "What's all this, Matt?"

"Just the incoming classified material, Mr. Wells."

Wells groaned as Colonel Howe deposited the papers in the incoming file. "Oh, no! Matt, you can't *do* this to me!" he said.

"Sorry, sir, I hate to see it stack up on you," his aide

said, "but the classified traffic has been running a lot heavier lately."

"I know. That situation briefing this morning wasn't very reassuring, was it?"

"No, sir. It reminded me a lot of the storm signals we were getting just before the Japs hit Pearl Harbor."

"Right. I had exactly the same feeling—especially about the deterioration in the personnel situation. Unless this trend is reversed—and soon—we'll be inviting the buzzards to hit us before we can mount even the semblance of a reprisal attack."

Colonel Howe looked glum. He was a career officer, whose West Point rigidity had been tempered by five thousand hours of military flying, including twenty-one unescorted bombing missions before his B-17 was shot down by the first of the German jet fighter attacks. Now forty-two and balding slightly, he was also putting on a bit of weight that made him chafe at the inaction of a desk job. The Air Force was his whole life, and anything which adversely affected its efficiency made him feel wretched.

Secretary Wells smiled. "Cheer up, Matt. Tomorrow you can get in a bit of stick time, and after you've kicked that new jet job around for a while, you'll feel human again."

Colonel Howe grinned appreciatively. Once a week, at least, he could get back into a parachute harness. The crows'-feet around his eyes twinkled at the thought.

"Meanwhile," Wells said, "we've got to get you some more help with your paper-work, if you want to keep getting in your flight time. Now, about that Special Assistant vacancy on my staff: have you screened any more applicants?"

"Yes, sir. I've just finished talking to a candidate who looks good. Here's his résumé."

"I notice you say 'candidate' instead of 'applicant.' I hope that means he's not one of the political hacks who've been panting outside my door for the past month, but someone we sought out instead."

"That's right, sir. This one is different. I didn't even know he was available, or I'd have been after him weeks ago."

"Who is he, and what's his background?"

"I don't believe you know him, sir. His name's Brett Cable, and he's an ex-Marine—a reserve Colonel with extensive public information experience before the war and a tour of staff public relations duty afterward."

"Sounds like he's heavy on the staff side. You know my requirement for combat experience for anyone assigned to Military Morale. Has he had any?"

"Yes, sir. He was squadron commander of an outstanding carrier-based Marine Corps fighter squadron operating off a CVL with Corsairs. He shot down nine enemy planes and has five combat decorations, including the DFC. More than half of the pilots in his squadron became aces."

"Another aviator, eh, Matt? You wouldn't be prejudiced in favor of fighter pilots, would you?"

Colonel Howe grinned. "Well, maybe. But I know the breed. They can carry out an assignment, and they can work alone—which he'll have to do under our setup."

"That's right. It'll be a one-man job, just like the other Special Assistant assignments. I'm not going to be tagged as an empire builder. All he'll get is a secretary, and no matter how heavy the work-load becomes, we can't give him an assistant."

"He understands that, sir, and it won't bother him—if we can get him."

"Don't worry about that. We can always spring him, can't we?"

"That's the catch, sir. He's not on active duty."

"A civilian, eh? And all tied up with some commercial firm that pays him a lot more than the government can afford?"

"No, sir. As a matter of fact, he's not working just now. And he's not sure he wants this job."

The Secretary's eyebrows raised. "For a man out of work, he sounds pretty choosy. Did you talk salary with him?"

"No, sir. I knew you wanted either a colonel who could be sprung for the job, or a top-notch professional we could bring in as a GS-15 or -16. But he didn't want to talk salary until he'd talked to you and got your personal slant on the job."

"That sounds reasonable," Wells said, opening the manila folder on his desk. "Now, let's see what he says about himself. A good State University, A.B. in journalism, newspaperman—Baltimore *Star,* an excellent newspaper. Magazine experience—non-fiction, thank Heaven; I don't want any ex-novelists around here, with all the speeches he'll have to grind out. Ah! He's had a tour of duty in the Pentagon, which gives him a six-months' edge on anyone who hasn't. Where did you latch onto him, Matt?"

"The National Committee sent his name over. He was on the President's press train during the last election, and they say he did a top-notch job. They tried to hire him afterward, but he took an airline job instead."

"No political ambitions, eh? Well, at least he's on the

right side politically, as far as this Administration is concerned. And that's one less check we'd have to run on him. How about the reference, credit, and name-checks?"

"I've already run those, sir. He's okay on all counts."

Secretary Wells glanced at the folder again.

"Hmm! Forty-six years old. This must be an old photograph, or else a retouched one."

"No, sir; it was taken just last week. He's in good shape, and looks a good deal younger than I do."

The Secretary eyed his aide reproachfully. "You're forty-two, Matt, and you look a good deal younger than I do at forty! What's this fellow's secret of eternal youth, anyhow?"

"Well, sir, his wife is twelve years younger than he is, and she's a knockout. He met her in Australia, at the start of the war. They're the happiest couple I've ever met, with the nicest children I ever saw."

"Hmm. Three children, age twelve, ten, and eight. Boy, girl, boy—each two years apart. That's what I call spacing by the book. His wife's blonde and buxom, I suppose?"

"No, sir. A natural red-head, with a teen-age figure."

"You've met her, then?"

"We've had them to dinner twice. My wife likes her a lot."

"That's in his favor. A pretty wife who's liked by other women is a priceless asset—in business, at least."

"The same in military life, sir. A lot of service wives have kept their husbands wearing silver eagles instead of silver stars, and *vice-versa*."

"Right you are. Now, let's see—his last job: Two years as Public Relations Director, Central American Division of International Airlines. Reason for leaving: tropical climate too hard on children's health, plus inadequate educational facilities. Well, he'll not find the school situation much better up here, I'm afraid, but at least he's shown some parental responsibility." He closed the folder and sat back in his chair. "Now, Matt, how would you describe Colonel Brett Cable, in a few well-chosen words?"

Colonel Howe glanced at a sheet from a memorandum pad. "Here's what his last employers told me: 'he's a team player, a thorough and persistent researcher, an expert in mass communications. We're sorry to lose him.' On the military side, his last four fitness reports rate him outstanding and place him in the top ten per cent, and his last c.o. described him as an outstanding officer in every respect and a real trouble-shooter in a crisis. From my standpoint, he's got all the other applicants I've interviewed in the past six weeks outclassed by a country mile."

The Secretary grinned. "And on top of that, he has a pretty wife. All right, Matt, I won't make your job any harder than I have to. If you think Brett Cable can fill the bill as my Special Assistant for Public Relations, I'll be glad to talk to him any time you can set it up. How's my calendar?"

"The best we can do is next Friday morning between eight and eight-fifteen. If you want more time, it'll have to be the following week."

"Fifteen minutes is plenty. If I want more time with him I'll have him out to the house some evening after dinner. My wife can look him over, and I want to see that red-headed wife of his, who seems to have made such an impression on you. Thank you, Matt."

He handed the folder back to Colonel Howe, and both men smiled understandingly.

CHAPTER TWO

Brett Cable, Recruit

Ten days later, at seven-thirty on a summer morning late in August, Brett Cable drove up the ramp to the Mall entrance of the Pentagon. The day was already warm and humid with heat waves shimmering from the tops of the myriad automobiles that were pouring into the large parking areas.

Previous familiarity with the scarcity of parking space for visitors prompted Brett to arrive a full half-hour before his appointment. Nearly thirty thousand people—military personnel and civilian employees of the armed services and the Department of Defense—arrived each morning by car or bus, most of them in car pools. Only those who arrived early, even though they held the coveted "S" permits for parking in the limited number of special parking spaces, could hope to park within easy walking distance of the vast gray building; those who arrived at the end of the rush hour were relegated to the outskirts of the parking areas, a fifteen-minute walk in the hot sun.

Visitors who asked for parking instructions were peremptorily directed to the outer parking lots by the traffic officers on duty at the Mall and River entrances, unless they were obviously very important persons, in which case they were courteously escorted to parking spaces directly in front of one of the main entrances.

Brett knew all about this procedure, and how to circumvent it. The four-year-old sedan he had recently purchased from a used-car dealer was brightly polished, giving it the appearance of a much more recent model. Driving boldly up to the traffic officer who stood on the front steps, Brett began the exchange he knew had worked before.

"Officer," he said, "I've got an appointment with Secretary Wells, which you can verify through his aide, Colonel Howe. May I park in that empty space there?"

He pointed to one of the special parking spaces, and the officer scowled, knowing that any visitor had the right to request permission to park there on urgent business.

"What room is he in?" the officer asked. He knew the room number of every Pentagon official who rated a government limousine.

Brett knew this challenge was coming, and his answer was prompt. "Room three E nine-sixty."

"How long will you be?"

"At least an hour," Brett said, knowing that a request for a shorter visit would receive a curt refusal.

The officer glared skeptically. "All right. You can park there this time. But after this, go to the Visitors' Parking Area in lanes twelve and thirteen, South Parking."

"Thanks, officer," Brett said. He knew that these lanes were always filled with a lineup of cars whose drivers sometimes had to wait more than half an hour for a parking space.

The officer wrote out a parking permit, which Brett knew was good for two hours, and stuck it under the windshield wiper.

Brett parked his car and walked up the limestone steps

past the bronze bust of Secretary Forrestal and into the airconditioned comfort of the Pentagon. The soft indirect lighting was a welcome relief from the glare of the morning sun outside.

Turning left into the first corridor, he walked down around the first turn and into the Office of Public Relations of the Department of Defense, where each of the armed services had representatives. Just inside the door was the section assigned to the U.S. Marine Corps. At the desk sat Major Joe Tuttle, U.S.M.C., a square-shouldered man with a crew haircut and two rows of well-starred combat ribbons under his aviator's wings.

Major Tuttle looked up as Brett entered. "Why, hello, Colonel Cable! Long time no see! What brings you back?" He stood up and gave Brett a hearty handshake.

"I'm just another civilian, Tutt, seeking some information. How's everything here in OPR since I was sitting in that hot seat just after the war?"

"Same old rat-race. What can I help you with?"

"I need a biographical summary of one of the Assistant Secretaries. Can do?"

"Sure thing. Which one?"

"Wells, of Military Morale. What kind of a guy is he?"

"He's tops. Knows his job and always clears everything through channels, instead of by-passing and free-wheeling like some of the other Secretaries are inclined to do," Major Tuttle said. He leafed through a filing cabinet and handed Brett a mimeographed sheet. "Here you are: J. Hardy Wells, ASDMM. Say, you're not coming back on active duty again, are you, I hope?"

"No such luck, Tutt. Not without flight pay, at least. And they can't afford that for Reservists, these days. Why, what makes you ask?"

"Because Secretary Wells is trying to find a Special

Assistant for Public Relations, and wants someone with experience like yours."

"I know. I'm on my way up to see him about the job—as a civilian."

Major Tuttle looked startled. "As a *civilian?* Say, that's a *good* idea. Nobody could pull rank on you, even with four stars. Golly, what an ideal setup! That office sure could use somebody who knows something about clearances and deadlines, with all the speeches he makes. His aide, Colonel Howe, makes a stab at it, but he's swamped, like everybody else in that office."

"So Wells makes a lot of speeches?"

"You said it. He's always on the go. I sure hope you take that job, Colonel."

"If I do, Tutt, you'll have to stop calling me 'Colonel.' "

"Okay, Colonel Cable, sir. From now on, I hope I'll be calling you 'Mister.' "

"Thanks, Tutt. And thanks for all the dope and the biography."

"Not at all, Brett, and good luck to you."

On his way up the escalator, Brett scanned the mimeographed data on the biography sheet. By the time he reached Room 3E960 he had memorized all the major milestones in the career of the man he was about to meet for the first time.

Colonel Howe ushered him into the office of Secretary Wells, who rose to meet him.

Wells smiled and extended his hand. "I'm glad to see you, Colonel Cable. Here, let's sit down over there where we can be more comfortable." He led the way to a glass-topped serving table between two leather-covered davenports. "Cigarette? I'm afraid all I can offer you are these I picked up last week during an inspection trip to the

Philippines. You may find them a bit strong, and they're probably dry." He extended the pack to Brett, took one himself, and held out a lighter. "Coffee?" he asked Brett.

"Thank you, I'd like some," Brett said.

Wells poured two cups of coffee from a thermos jug. Both men drank it black.

"I've been through your background summary," Wells said, "and you've made quite an impression on Matt Howe. He's a good officer, and I trust his judgment. We need someone with your background, but I don't want to minimize the problems we face. This is a tough job. We're understaffed, and we always will be—in peace-time, at least. The only way we can make up for it is through hard work and long hours. The rest of my staff takes these conditions for granted. I work best under pressure, and there's plenty of it here. I just want you to know what you'd be up against, from the start, so far as working conditions are concerned."

"This is good coffee, Mr. Wells," Brett said. "I don't think I'd have any trouble staying awake on the job, and I'm used to meeting deadlines."

Wells smiled, and relaxed visibly. "Good. I see we understand each other. Now, let me tell you a bit about our problems. We're right in the middle of the worst military manpower crisis this country's ever known—worse than the headlong demobilization after World War Two, even worse than during the Korean War when our troops were very nearly driven into the sea and were saved only by MacArthur's fantastic gamble in the amphibious landings at Inchon. At the rate we're losing our best trained personnel, we'll go broke trying to maintain our peace-time forces overseas—without even being able to strike back when the enemy hits us."

"Excuse me, Mr. Wells," Brett said, "but I noticed a

choice of words I've never heard used by a government official—except in war-time. Do you mind if I ask you a couple of pretty blunt questions?"

"Not at all. Go right ahead."

"Well, I noticed you said '*the* enemy'—which is a limiting phrase—rather than the term 'our enemies' which we used during the last two wars. I've been out of the country for the past two years, and I didn't realize we'd narrowed it down to such an extent. Is the term 'the enemy' in general use—publicly, I mean?"

"Yes, it is—not only publicly, but officially. In World War Two we were fighting the Berlin-Rome-Tokyo Axis Powers. In Korea we were fighting troops of two nations—the North Koreans and the Chinese Communists. Today we make no bones about who the real enemy is and where his headquarters are—the only possible enemy who can and would attack our cities with nuclear weapons—the USSR, whose Pentagon is the Kremlin."

"Soviet Russia, then, is *the* enemy?"

"Soviet Communism. Our official position is that we have no quarrel with the *peoples* of Russia, but only with their Communist masters, who have openly proclaimed their objective of world conquest through violent revolution."

Brett paused thoughtfully for a moment. "Then," he said, "I also noticed that you said *when* the enemy attacks us, rather than using the word *if*. That's pretty strong language, when we're talking about an all-out attack with atomic weapons. Does it mean what I'd have to assume it meant if I saw it in a public statement attributed to a man in your position?"

Wells looked searchingly into Brett's eyes for several seconds, then said very quietly, "Yes, it does, Mr. Cable.

It also tells me a lot about you and your respect for the English language. I wish someone like you were riding herd on several of our top government spokesmen whose public statements often sound as though they were issued after being dictated but not read. Are you always as precise in your semantic reactions?"

"I'm afraid so, Mr. Wells—especially if I'm writing for publication under someone else's by-line—which is the way I earn my living."

Wells placed his fingertips together and glanced out of the window, pursing his lips as though whistling inaudibly in silent thought. After a moment he turned back to Brett. "Mr. Cable," he said, "I'm going to be very frank with you—perhaps more than I should. But time's too short, and I'll come right to the point by telling you what we're up against. What I'm about to tell you is information affecting the security of the United States. You know what that means. Do you accept the responsibilities that go along with access to such information?"

"Yes, Mr. Wells. I know the penalties for revealing Security Information to unauthorized persons. If you think it's necessary to my understanding of the situation, go ahead."

"Good. Well, here's how we stand. Before World War Two, we had approximately half a million officers and men in our Armed Services. Today we have six times as many—more than three million men—the largest stand-by force in the nation's history. And the cost per man has skyrocketed appallingly. To train you as a pilot cost around thirty thousand dollars, and the planes you flew in combat cost around a hundred thousand apiece. Today it costs six hundred thousand dollars to train a pilot for a jet bomber that costs eight million dollars."

Brett's eyes widened, and Wells continued: "The planes not only cost eighty times more than they did, but they're far more complicated: a three-man jet bomber's wiring system alone is as complex as that of a good-sized city. To maintain the electronic equipment and armament on one of these planes takes the average enlisted technician about three years to learn, out of a four-year enlistment, and by that time industry is bidding ten times his military pay for his services in a civilian capacity. As a result, we're losing our best men in droves—officers as well as enlisted men. Just before the Korean War in 1950 the Air Force's re-enlistment rate was around 55 per cent; today it's only 22. Even the Marine Corps' re-enlistments have shrunk from 35 per cent to 19. The other services are in much worse shape. The Army's rate has slumped from 62 per cent to 12, and the Navy's from 66 per cent to an all-time low of only 8 per cent. During the past six months only 71,000 out of 500,000 eligible men re-enlisted, so that we lost 429,000 trained men whose services must be replaced. Today we're spending more than 65 per cent of our national budget for defense—and losing about 85 per cent of our trained manpower *every year.* No country on earth can long afford such a constant drain on its finances."

Brett shook his head in shocked disbelief. "Why are they quitting? What's behind it?"

Wells replied in French: *"Cherchez la femme; c'est toujours la femme. Comprenez-vous?"*

"Ça juste," Brett answered. *"Mais, pourquois?* I was married, and I served twenty years."

"I know, but there are many more complicating factors today. The men marry younger. Their wives are younger. Most professional soldiers and sailors in the old days were bachelors until they were past thirty, but not any more. Life was much simpler in those days—and much less expensive. Then there's the decline in *esprit de corps,* and in the public's support of and respect for its fighting men."

"Which came first, and what caused it?"

"Those are good questions. I wish I knew the answers. We've got to find out, and take corrective steps—fast. If we don't, we're sunk. I intend to get the facts and lay them before the public; my success or failure in this assignment depends almost entirely on how successful I am in doing so. That's why I need your help, Mr. Cable."

"That sounds like an offer."

"It is, and I hope you will accept it. To give you just one indication of the seriousness of the situation, I can tell you that I've been authorized to offer the right man a GS-16 rating—and I think you're the right man."

"I'm not familiar with the civilian ratings, Mr. Wells. What does it compare with on the military scale?"

"It's in the so-called super-grade category. In responsibility, it's roughly the equivalent of the military rank of Brigadier General. The starting pay is twelve thousand dollars a year."

"When would you want me to start?"

"As soon as possible. I've got four major speeches scheduled, and I'm leaving a week from today to check on the morale situation at our bases in the mid-East. I'd have to know your answer within a week at the latest."

"I'll let you know within twenty-four hours."

Secretary Wells grinned broadly and held out his hand. "Thank you for that, Mr. Cable. I really appreciate such a vote of confidence. By the way, would it be convenient for you and your wife to drop in on me and Mrs. Wells tonight after dinner for a drink? I'd ask you over for cocktails and dinner, but I'm never home in time, and I usually eat here instead."

"We'd be delighted to come."

"Fine," Wells said, showing Brett to the door. "We'll expect you, then, about eight-thirty. Goodbye, Mr. Cable, and thank you again for coming. I hope you'll soon be here with us as a member of our team."

"Thank you, Mr. Wells," Brett said. "We'll see you tonight."

CHAPTER THREE

An Estimate of the Situation

After leaving the office of Secretary Wells, Brett stopped off to thank Colonel Howe, then headed for the nearest public telephone booth in one of the Pentagon corridors to telephone his wife.

"Hello, darling," he said. "He offered me the job."

"I knew he would," Jane said. "How could anyone refuse you anything?"

"But I didn't ask him. He asked me to take it."

"Of course he would. Did you accept?"

"Not yet, my love. This is something we've got to decide together. The responsibilities are enormous, and there are lots of complications—unlike anything we've ever faced before. I'll tell you all about it when I come home. But first I'm going to do a bit of outside checking, so please don't expect me for dinner. I may be late."

"All right, dear. I'll try to be patient, but I'm dying to hear all the details."

"We're invited over for drinks and to meet his wife at eight-thirty. Can you make it?"

"Of course, I'll arrange everything. What should I wear, and what can I lay out for you to wear?"

"Wear something cool, and will you please lay out my lightweight dark suit, a white shirt, and pick me out a tie to go with it."

"Certainly, darlingest. I'll have everything set when you come home. And don't forget to eat. I love you!"

"I love you more. Goodbye for now."

Brett walked down an interior stairway to the first floor and along the corridor until he came to a sign labeled *Military Intelligence Division of the Department of Defense. Restricted Area.* A Military Policeman with a white helmet stood at the door, behind a WAC Lieutenant at the reception desk. The girl glanced up casually at Brett, blinked her eyes, then smiled as she looked at him with unconcealed appreciation. "Can I help you, sir?" she asked.

"I'd like to see Colonel Gilbert Morrison," Brett said. "I believe he's on duty here in MID."

"I'm sorry, sir, but he's on convalescent leave at the Federal Hospital. You could call him there, if it's important. I can ring him for you, if you like."

"Would you, please? I'd appreciate it."

The girl dialed a number, and Brett soon had his old friend Gib Morrison on the telephone. They had flown Corsairs together in the same squadron, until one day off Guadalcanal when Gib had been shot down with a shattered arm which had to be amputated. Brett had followed him down, splashing the Jap Zero which had machine-gunned Gib as he dangled helplessly in his parachute.

Gib was now recuperating from a corrective operation to eliminate complications resulting from his hastily patched-up battle wounds.

"Nothing serious," he reassured Brett, "they only had to trim off another inch or so, and I've got a better stump than I had before. Come on over, you old war-horse, and tell me what you're up to."

Twenty minutes later, Brett and Gib were strolling on

the sun-deck of the Federal Hospital. By contrast with Brett, Gib was frail and gaunt. The sleeve of his dressing-gown was neatly pinned up under the stump of his left arm. He listened attentively while Brett described his meeting with Secretary Wells.

"We talked less than ten minutes," Brett said, "and even before we were half-way through, he was doing most of the selling. That tells me one thing for sure: he's anxious to fill a hot seat, but no one who could qualify has been willing to take it on. Why?"

"Well, from what you've told me, Brett, he didn't pull any punches about how critical the situation really is—at least from his viewpoint. He's trying to carry out an almost impossible assignment."

"Right. He used the old technique of telling me how tough the job was, to see if I'd accept it as a challenge."

"And you rose to the bait—as you've always done whenever there's a good fight anywhere."

"Yes, but I haven't swallowed it yet. Gib, he told me a lot more—purposely—than I had a right to hear until I'm cleared again for classified information. But that's only one side of the picture—our side. What I need now, in order to make an intelligent decision, is to have some idea of how the other side stacks up. You've been on duty in M.I.D., and I won't embarrass you by asking you for an estimate of the situation. But can you give me any unclassified indicators that don't come under the category of trade secrets? I've promised Wells I'd give him a yes-or-no answer by tomorrow morning."

Gib's eyes moistened. "Brett," he said, "you're a real patriot. Anyone else would have walked all around this thing, stalling Wells off for a week, and then would have shied away from it like it was poison ivy. If I didn't know you better, I'd think you were job-hungry; but I know a dozen outfits that would snap you up at half again as much as this job pays. Isn't that right?"

"I'm under no pressure," Brett admitted. "In fact, I'd planned to take Jane and the children up to the Cape for a month, before even starting to look around. But this thing disturbs me, Gib. I'd hate to see everything we fought for go down the drain."

"That's an apt expression, and that's just about what's happening. The plug has already been pulled, and anyone who listens with half an ear can hear the loud, sucking noise in the center of the whirlpool. Come along down to my room, Brett, and I'll show you why you shouldn't take that job—or at least convince you how futile it would be."

Brett eyed him quizzically, and Gib chuckled. "Same old Brett," he said. "You old varmint. You never did scare very easily."

"I've been scared before—plenty—and you know it. Frankly, I'm scared right now, just thinking over what Wells told me an hour ago."

"Thank God," Gib said fervently. "If a few more people like you could be scared in the same way, we might beat the buggers yet."

Gib had a large, airy room overlooking the Potomac River. "We don't even need to close the door for this briefing," he said. "Everything I'm going to tell you is already in print, right there on that table." He pointed to a stack of magazines and newspapers beside his high, wheeled bed. "I read 'em all," he said, "on both sides of the fence—including the *Daily Worker*. Let's see, now, you've been away for about two years. Can you still name the two major political groups in the United States?"

Brett looked startled. "Why, the Democrats and the Republicans, I suppose. Don't they far outnumber all others?"

"Not any more, Junior. Those are only 'fronts' for voting purposes. There's a different lineup today, which crosses all regular party lines. Today most Americans can be classified into two major political groups—the Liberals and the Conservatives. There are Liberal Republicans and Conservative Democrats, for example. And, just to confuse you, today neither word means what it used to mean," he said, picking up a copy of *Webster's Collegiate Dictionary*. "First let's take the word *liberal,* in the political sense, which is defined as 'specifically, having a tendency toward democratic or republican, as distinguished from monarchial or aristocratic forms.' Now let's look at *conservative.* Here we are: 'designating, pertaining to, or characteristic of a political party which favors the conservation of existing institutions and forms of government.' Do you follow me?"

"So far, yes. But I ought to warn you that I'm a babe in the woods, politically. I thought you were going to tell me we'd revived something like the Bull Moose Party."

"No such luck. That's much too simple for us. We've got to complicate it all over the lot, instead of simplifying it, like our unworthy opponents in this fracas. *They* only have *one* party."

"Which makes for quick decisions," Brett said, "like Pearl Harbor and Korea."

"And the Hungarian massacre and the Kremlin's atomic ultimatum to Britain and France which ended their invasion at Suez," Gib added bitterly, "while we twiddled our thumbs waiting for the United Nations to intervene—which it never did and never can do in time to be of any use to the country that's being gobbled up."

Brett looked thoughtful. "I'm afraid you're right."

"Good—so long as you stay afraid. Now, that brings us back to the chief difference between our two major political groups. The Conservatives *are* afraid—afraid to trust our sworn enemies who have boasted publicly that time is on their side and that they're going to bury us—afraid to trust paper promises made by mass murderers who have always violated their most solemn agreements—afraid of uncontrolled spending that will mean ruin to any nation just as surely as it does to any family or any business organization—afraid of phony peace overtures that would weaken our military defenses and leave us wide open for atomic annihilation . . ." Gib said, pausing for breath, "and a dozen other things that affect our national survival. Conservatives just want to stay alive, and to avoid selling their children into insolvency and slavery."

"How about the Liberals?" Brett asked.

"*They* aren't afraid of *anything*. Let's go back to the dictionary, and you'll see why they're called *Liberals*. Webster's lists seven definitions, including the one I read to you, which is number seven. Here we go: '1. Befitting a man of free birth; not restricted; as a *liberal* manner or education; 2. Bestowing in a large and noble way, generous; bounteous; openhanded. 3. Bestowed in a large way; hence, abundant; bountiful, ample. 4. *Archaic:* Free from restraint; unchecked; licentious.' Want any more?"

"That's plenty," Brett said. "Let's go back to the other definitions of *conservative*."

"Okay. There are only four, and I've already read you

the last one. Here are the first three: '1. Conserving, preservative. 2. Disposed to maintain existing institutions or views; opposed to change. 3. Within safe bounds; moderate; as, a *conservative* estimate; also, adhering to sound principles believed to involve little risk; as, a *conservative* investment.' Now, how does that sound to you, as compared with the giveaway group?"

"It sounds like a description of most aviators. You know: 'There are old pilots and bold pilots, but there are no old bold pilots.' Remember?"

"Right," Gib said. "Also, 'never give away anything that you need to survive—especially your altitude advantage or your flying speed.' We've buried a lot of our friends who ignored that one—those we could find afterwards."

"All right, Professor. I'm beginning to see daylight. Now, which are there more of—Conservatives or Liberals?"

"*You* tell *me*. How many people prefer pie in the sky, so long as someone else foots the bill?"

"Good Lord, no!" Brett said. "Don't tell me it's *that* bad!"

"You've forgotten your flight statistics. What was the rate of attrition in our class of one hundred aviation cadets?"

Brett thought for a moment. "Let's see, about sixty washed out in flight training . . ."

"How would you classify them—Liberal or Conservative?"

"Well, they certainly weren't conservative enough in their flying to convince their instructors that they could be trusted with military aircraft."

"Go ahead," Gib said. "I'll keep count."

"Then there were five who were killed in training accidents—usually due to pilot error."

"That leaves thirty. Now, how many of those were operational or combat casualties, including me?"

"Let's see, about a dozen were killed, three were missing in action, and five are wearing Purple Hearts," Brett said.

"That leaves ten—only ten per cent of our original group who survived unscathed."

"You mean they're the only ones you'd call conservative?"

"Let's put it this way," Gib said. "They were at least more successful than the rest of us in staying within safe bounds, adhering to sound principles, and conserving or preserving their own lives and the equipment they were entrusted with—all good conservative traits. Isn't that the best way to maintain our existing institutions and our traditions and our religious views? Isn't that the best way to oppose changes we don't want—like a change of our national language from English to Japanese or German or Russian?"

"Well, yes, if you're talking about war."

"That's exactly what we're talking about. They may call it a 'cold war,' but those nose-diving re-enlistment figures are a pretty good indication of how close it's getting to the boiling point," Gib said.

"You mean the boys are getting out because they're afraid there's a squall coming?"

"No, it's the other way around. There's so much prosperity and so much peace talk they just can't see any future in military life. Of course, that's just a smoke-screen —aided and abetted by the Liberal writers, editors and publishers, who are far and away in the majority, and who have swallowed the current Communist Party line of 'peaceful co-existence.' "

"What about the Conservatives?" Brett asked. "I should think they'd be yelling their heads off."

"They do, but true Conservatives are as scarce—percentage-wise—as pilots who become aces without getting shot up in the process. And they're bucking one of the stubbornest traits of human nature: people just don't like to hear bad news. Even when disaster strikes, most people refuse to believe it, like the poor devils who ignore the hurricane warnings until they see water knee-deep on their living-room floors. Remember how long it took to convince our forces at Pearl Harbor that they were actually being attacked, even with the loud-speakers blaring, 'Those are enemy planes! This is no drill!' That's just the way it's going today: the storm warnings are up all around us, but very few people even bother to read them."

Gib paused, and held up a blue-backed magazine. "Here's a good example. This outfit has been sounding the general alarm for months, giving facts and figures, but they've been ridiculed as just a bunch of calamity-howlers. Yet nobody can challenge these facts, which are common public knowledge: Germany nearly won both World Wars right at the beginning with submarine warfare. She had only 57 U-boats at the start of the second World War, and they damned near knocked England out of the fight before we got into it. Now, take a look at how many the Soviets could throw at us tomorrow—475 modern, high-speed subs—twice as fast as anything the Nazis had, and armed with atomic torpedoes and guided missiles that can be launched from 100 miles at sea and still hit any city within 200 miles of our coasts."

"Ouch," Brett said, wincing visibly. "That's more than eight times the size of Hitler's submarine fleet."

"That's right. And what made old Adolf decide not to launch his amphibious invasion of England?"

"The British Navy," Brett replied. "He decided to let the Luftwaffe do the job, and the Royal Air Force spoiled his plans."

"Right. And where are the Royal Navy and the R.A.F. today?"

"In mothballs, I suppose, just like most of our ships and planes."

"Wrong," Gib said. "You should go to the foot of the class. You've been out of the country too long. The Royal Navy's being scrapped, and the . . ."

"Scrapped? You can't mean actually . . ."

"That's right. I said *scrapped.* And so is the Royal Air Force, which is converting almost completely to nuclear-armed missiles. And that's what the Soviets are doing, and that's what we're doing, as fast as we can make the change-over."

"My God!" Brett said. "It's hard to believe."

"I know, 'it can't happen here.' But it has. At the rate we're going, everybody in uniform will end up in some branch of a kind of glorified field artillery equipped with long-range rocket launchers that can be fired from planes, tanks, ships, or submarines."

"How long has this been going on, for Pete's sake?"

"About eighteen years. A V-2 rocket got away from the Germans back in 1941 and landed in Sweden. A modified V-1 was launched from one of our subs just after the war at a good-sized task force two hundred miles away, and flew right through the center of everything we could throw up at it, without being knocked down. A Snark launched recently in Florida ended up three thousand miles away in Brazil."

"Wow!" Brett said. "There'll be no place to hide."

"You said it. Look at this poll: two out of every five persons living in England would leave the country if they could, and those who can are emigrating to Canada and Australia at the rate of ten thousand a month. England, Holland, Germany, Norway, Denmark, Spain, Turkey, and Japan have been threatened with attack by Soviet atomic rockets if they permit U.S. guided missile bases to be installed on their territory or accept the delivery of atomic weapons."

"How did the public react to that news?"

"You can judge for yourself from this news item: After our last nationwide Civil Defense drill, it was estimated that only one out of every five persons would bother to take shelter in the event of a *real* enemy attack."

"What about the Civil Defense authorities?"

Gib laughed mirthlessly. "Here's the verdict on that from the Congressional Committee that rides herd on government appropriations: 'Civil defense plans are a farce. Every cent spent to date has been a waste of public funds. The Civil Defense Administration has been grossly negligent in continuing emphasis on mass-evacuation in the event of an H-bomb attack. Highway improvements alone would cost nearly twenty-eight billion dollars under any plan to move the population of 147 primary target areas 40 miles in two and a half hours.' Get that, now: twenty-eight *billion* bucks—nearly half as much as our whole national budget! And guess what they proposed instead—as an 'economy' measure."

"Read on," Brett said, gloomily.

"They said that in view of the overwhelming evidence

that mass evacuation of cities and suburban areas is unworkable, it would be 'cheaper and safer' to build shelters for 135 *million* people."

"How much would *that* cost?"

"Only twenty billion bucks—just enough to ruin the country without even firing a shot—that's all."

"Are they *all* batty?"

"Nope. One Conservative Congressman spoke up and suggested that we'd be foolish to spend ourselves into bankruptcy before we even know what form the next war will take—a war which, he said, we may be able to avoid if we first think and act in the interests of our own country."

"He ought to run for President," Brett said.

"He'd lose even if he could get himself nominated. He's not the spending kind. And the Liberals would tear him apart."

"Gib, you're a cynic."

"No, I'm just a realist."

"Do you really think they're going to hit us?"

"What for? Why should they? They can't do it now without getting hurt in return. We've always got some of our strategic bombers in the air, carrying live but unarmed atomic bombs."

"Whew! Has *that* been published?"

Gib picked up a newspaper. "Here you are. Read it yourself."

Brett shook his head speechlessly as he read the news item.

"There's your answer," Gib said. "Why risk direct military action, when you can get everything you want without even firing a shot? Just look at the box score. In 1903 Lenin established the Communist Party with just seventeen supporters. In 1917, 40,000 Communists destroyed the new-born Republic of Russia and enslaved 150 million people. Today there are 193 million people in the USSR. Since V-J Day, China and fifteen other countries with 725 million people have been swallowed up the same way. Today there are 918 million people under the complete domination of those who have sworn to destroy us—and today we stand alone as the only major power in the free world. Why should they risk an attack, when all they have to do is to wait for us to drop in their lap like an over-ripe plum?"

"I notice you said 'wait' instead of 'sit and wait.' Obviously they're not sitting still."

"Hell, no. They're busier than a hive of bees, and as active as termites, sawing away at our foundations."

"How many are there in this country?"

"One FBI informer reported 3,800 in his area, in eastern Pennsylvania and Delaware, mostly in the steel industry. Another witness testified that he and a group of twenty Party members engineered a strike of 9,000 workers in New Jersey which cost the workers, the company, and the local community 54 million dollars."

"What are their chief tools? Sabotage?"

"Not openly. Not yet. But it's all set to start when the whistle blows. Until then, they'll keep on with 'cold war' tactics—especially psychological and economic warfare—to weaken us for the kill. Right now, we're spending more on our 'cold war' defenses than it cost us to lick the Japs."

"What are their chief targets?" Brett asked.

"The personnel of the Armed Services which we'd use first to retaliate: the Air Force and the Navy. They'll do everything they can to undercut, demoralize and weaken us there—especially our Navy. They're great students of history, and they hate and fear the Navy, which has been the decisive factor in every war we've fought and won. They've got a healthy respect for our sea-air power."

"So that's it," Brett said, reflectively. "Well, that figures. The Navy's re-enlistment rate is the lowest, which shows where they're concentrating their efforts. No wonder Secretary Wells can't get anyone to take that job he just offered me."

Gib grinned at him impishly.

"Don't look at *me* that way!" Brett said.

"You want to bet?"

"Not on your life. Not after what you've shown me, right where everyone can read it—including the enemy."

"Let's have a drink," Gib said, pressing a push-button on his bedside table. "They make me drink two ounces of bonded bourbon three times a day."

"*Make* you drink it? I've never seen you protest too much in the old days."

An attractive blonde nurse entered and said, "Yes, Colonel Morrison?"

"Time for my pick-me-up," Gib said. "And please bring one for my guest, too, Honey."

"Now, Colonel, you *know* that's against regulations," the nurse said. She glanced at Brett appreciatively, and hesitated.

"Don't worry, Prettykins," Gib said. "Colonel Cable's also a Marine. We fit the wah together, and I wouldn't be here now if it wasn't for him. Besides that, he's a V.I.P.I.—a Very Important Person Indeed. He's about to accept a top-drawer assignment in the Pentagon."

"Gib! Cut it out, please!" Brett protested.

The nurse left and came back with two drinks. After

she departed, Gib raised his glass. "Here's to you and your new job, Brett!" he said.

"You really think I'm fool enough to accept it, don't you?"

"You can't fool me, you derned old Conservative!"

"All right," Brett said, resignedly. He touched his glass to Gib's, took a sip, and sighed, "What a pair of salesmen I've run into today!"

"You'd already decided to take that job when I first saw you," Gib retorted.

"You've always been a pretty good judge of men, fast horses, good-looking gals, and fine whiskey," Brett admitted.

Gib took another swallow and smacked his lips. "Nasty old stuff," he said. "Wish I had a barrel of it!"

CHAPTER FOUR

Eileen Emery

As they drove toward Georgetown to meet Secretary and Mrs. Wells, Brett outlined the situation to his wife, without undue emphasis on the military aspects.

Jane listened quietly until he had finished, then said, "Brett, I want you to do what you think is right—not for you or for me, but for the children. And neither you nor your family can survive, if our country goes under. Neither of us could sleep at night if we dodged our responsibilities now."

"Thank you, darling. That's just the way I feel, too. I'm only sorry about upsetting our plans. We'll have to cancel our trip to the Cape."

"I know, Brett, but I don't mind. What if you were going away again for another three or four years overseas? At least we'll be together—which makes all the difference in the world."

"You're right, my love, as usual. No man ever had finer support than you've always given me."

"I love you, Brett, and I like you, too."

Brett braked the car to a stop at the side of the road, looked into his wife's green eyes, and gently kissed her. They drove on in silence, and she held his right hand tightly in both of hers.

Two hours later, they were on their way home after a very pleasant evening with Secretary and Mrs. Wells.

"I like her a lot," Jane said. "She's sweet and unassuming and hasn't let her husband's position go to her head."

"She liked you too," Brett said. "She told me so, while you were talking to him. How does he impress you?"

"I like him, Brett. If I'd had any qualms before, they'd be gone now. You'll enjoy working with a man like that. I'm glad you told him tonight that you'd take the job. We'll sleep better—and so will he."

Promptly at eight o'clock the next morning Brett was sworn in by Secretary Wells, with Colonel Howe as a witness. Brett held up his right hand and repeated the oath of office: "I solemnly swear that I will well and faithfully discharge the responsibilities and duties of the office I am about to accept, to the best of my abilities, and that I will defend and protect the Constitution of the United States of America against all enemies, foreign or domestic, so help me God."

"Congratulations," Wells said. "We're glad to have you with us."

"Thank you, Mr. Secretary," Brett said.

"You'll be in the room next to Colonel Howe's," Wells said. "I'll introduce you to the rest of the staff at our ten o'clock meeting. Matt will get you a parking permit and brief you on our office procedures. I believe he's already arranged for you to interview several secretaries from the Personnel Pool. Pick yourself a good one, because she'll be all the help we can give you. We'll see you later."

Brett's office was just big enough for two persons. There was only one window, but it looked out over the same majestic view that Secretary Wells enjoyed. The room had sound-absorbent panels in the ceiling and wall-to-wall carpeting—those hallmarks of prestige enjoyed in the Pentagon only by Admirals, Generals, and "super-grade" civilian officials.

On the executive-type desk next to the window was a folder with a slip of paper bearing the notation "For Mr. Cable." The other desk, smaller and containing a typewriter, was obviously for his secretary.

Seating himself in the well-padded swivel-chair, Brett opened the folder. Inside he found an organization chart and several memoranda on office procedures. One memorandum bore a blue card marked "SPECIAL ATTENTION." Brett noted the subject: "Completed Staff Work."

There was a knock at the door, and Colonel Howe entered the room.

"Hello, Brett. Mr. Wells wants to see you right away about some speeches he's working on." He glanced at the paper Brett was holding, and said, "That's all the indoctrination you'll need, if you just follow what's on that sheet. You're familiar with the Completed Staff Work principle, I'm sure."

"Right," Brett said, quoting from the document he held without looking at it: " 'Completed Staff Work is the study of a problem and presentation of a solution, by a staff officer, in such form that the head of the staff division has only to indicate his approval or disapproval of the recommended action . . . Don't worry your chief with long explanations and memoranda . . . Your views should be placed before him in completed form . . . If he wants comment or explanation, he'll ask for it . . . The final test is this: if you were the chief would you be willing to sign the paper you've prepared and stake your professional reputation on its being right? If not, don't even submit it, for its not Completed Staff Work.' "

Colonel Howe grinned. "I see the Marines didn't neglect your education."

"They wrote that definition," Brett said, "shortly before they introduced dive bombing—back when your outfit was still a branch of the Signal Corps!"

"Go ahead, rub it in! No wonder unification of the services is still just a dream. Nobody could ever absorb the Marine Corps; they'd end up running the show!"

Brett tucked a notebook into his side pocket, sharpened a black copy pencil, and went into the office of Secretary Wells.

"Please sit down," Wells said cordially. "I've got a couple of speeches here that need polishing up before they're released to the press. Will you please go over them and smooth out the rough spots? Matt tells me you're familiar with all the clearance procedures, which will be a big help. The multiple clearances we have to get before releasing anything for publication are among our biggest headaches—next to the requests I get for letters or statements endorsing various books and movies, for TV appearances, and so on. If you'll screen all such material for me and prepare replies for my signature, it'll be a tremendous help to me in cutting down the paper-work overload. Please use established facilities wherever you can; I don't want to build up a public relations operation of my own, but to utilize OPR and the public relations departments of the individual services."

Shortly afterward, the rest of the staff entered for the daily staff meeting. In addition to Brett, Secretary Wells had four other Special Assistants, including a Navy Captain, an Army Colonel, and two civilians who held GS-15 ratings. Wells addressed all of them by their first names, and the officers addressed him as "Mr. Wells." Brett and the two civilian assistants addressed him as "Mr. Secretary." Wells introduced Brett to the others, in a short, informal meeting at which everyone was completely at ease.

After the staff meeting, Colonel Howe handed Brett a folder containing the background résumés of applicants eligible to serve as Brett's private secretary—an assignment which carried the Civil Service rating of GS-7.

"After you look over these résumés," Matt said, "let me know which applicants you'd like to interview and we can set up the appointments. They're all available in the Personnel Pool."

Each summary, given in minute detail on the four-page Personnel Form 57, covered the applicant's background, education, and personal history. Brett eliminated all candidates without previous service in a public relations assignment, and set aside the applications of seven experienced secretaries. From previous experience in the Pentagon he knew that most of the secretaries available from the Personnel Pool were either misfits who could not carry out their assignments, or those who were dissatisfied with their rate of advancement. One girl's Form 57 listed qualifying experience so much more impressive than the others that it caught Brett's eye immediately. He took the form in to Colonel Howe. "Any dope on this one, Matt? Mrs. Emery. Judging from her résumé, she's got everything it takes."

Matt chuckled. "You said it, Brett. She sure has—and then some. But everyone who's interviewed her thinks twice about hiring her—and then changes his mind."

"Why? What's wrong with her?"

"You'll see when you interview her. But I'd suggest you talk to some of the others on your list before you interview Mrs. Emery. Then you'll see what I mean."

Brett did as Matt suggested, interviewing six other applicants first. Three were unimpressive, a fourth withdrew after reading the exacting job description, and the other two appeared capable of doing the work required. Brett then sent for the seventh applicant, Mrs. Eileen Emery. According to her personnel file, she was of Irish extraction, thirty years old, previously married and divorced, had no children, was five feet six inches tall, weighed one hundred and thirty pounds, and could type and take dictation faster than any of the other applicants.

Brett was absorbed in memorizing the organization chart when Mrs. Emery entered his office at the appointed time.

"Mr. Cable," she said, "I'm Mrs. Emery."

Brett swung around in his chair, looked up at her casually, and straightened up with a start. Their eyes met with something akin to an electric shock. She was strikingly attractive, with jet-black hair, dark brown eyes with long lashes and a figure like a pin-up model's.

For a moment Brett was speechless, until she dropped her eyes and blushed under his gaze.

He stood up quickly and said, "Excuse me, Mrs. Emery. I wasn't expecting you . . . to be . . . here . . . just yet. Please sit down." He glanced at the background summary on his desk. "You're apparently well qualified for a job like this. How do you happen to be in the Personnel Pool?"

She hesitated. "May I speak frankly, Mr. Cable?"

"Certainly. Please do."

"I can get plenty of jobs as a receptionist—where there's no real work and no responsibility. But I'm a trained secretary, and I want a decent job. The trouble is, once you've advanced as far as I have, most of the men you work for are executives in the super-grades—and most of them are married."

"Yes, I suppose that's right."

"I've worked for several of them and they all give the same reason when they tell me they'll have to change secretaries: they say that I work harder than anyone else, and that I've always kept our relationships on a strictly business basis—but that their wives just don't believe it."

"I can understand that," Brett said. "But don't let that worry you. My wife has green eyes, but she isn't jealous. What I need here is the best help I can get, in a job that has gone begging for months. Whoever comes in here will have all the work she can handle, and then some. I don't care whether she's ugly as sin or as pretty as you are, so long as we get the job done. Are you interested?"

"On that basis, yes. I'd be grateful for the chance."

"When can you start?"

"Right now."

"Good. There's a note pad. Please take a memorandum for Colonel Howe: 'Dear Matt: I see what you mean, and I still want the best-qualified secretary I can get. Accordingly, I've offered the job to Mrs. Emery, who can take dictation faster than you or I can talk, and she has accepted it. Sincerely yours, Brett Cable.' "

CHAPTER FIVE

Competition Appears

Brett quickly adjusted to his new assignment. Before a week had passed, Secretary Wells told Colonel Howe, "You certainly found the right man there, Matt. He's already justified his selection over anyone else who applied for the job."

Wells soon was leaning heavily on Brett for assistance in all public relations matters—speeches, press conferences, magazine articles, and television scripts. Whenever Wells left on one of his frequent inspection trips to overseas military installations, he asked Brett to represent him in the interminable succession of committee meetings and conferences which are the burden of every high Pentagon official.

Brett's "super-grade" classification carried many prerogatives, including a parking permit for the area reserved for government limousines and entry to the dining room reserved for Flag and General Officers, instead of having to stand in line with the Colonels and lesser officials who ate in the overcrowded Executive Dining Room. As one of the Secretary's acting deputies, he frequently sat in for Wells in conferences with Generals, Admirals, Assistant Secretaries, and the deputies of even higher officials.

For the first few days Brett took a bit of good-natured ribbing about his new secretary from Colonel Howe and his other associates. The Special Assistant for Legal Matters, a civilian who was also divorced, confided to Brett: "I'd have hired her in a second, if I'd thought I could get away with it. You're a brave man, Brett—or else you're made of stone, to be able to sit there with that buxom bundle of luscious femininity right in the same room with you. I'll always knock before I come in."

"You won't have to," Brett assured him. "One of the first rules for success in any public relations operation is to keep your office door open—as well as your eyes and ears. She's a good secretary."

"Well, Eileen's certainly an attractive addition to the office, in any case. Congratulations on your good judgment."

"Thanks a lot," Brett said. "I'll never keep her after hours, in case you're interested. And what she does in her spare time is her own business."

"Thanks, pal. I've already tried, but Eileen won't date anybody who works in the same building."

"That's a good rule. She's a smart girl—in more ways than one."

A few days later, Brett's brother, Ben, dropped by during a business trip through Washington. Ben, who was two years older than Brett, was a widower with a son in college and a daughter who was married and raising a family of her own. Ben had lived alone for the past three years since his wife's death. He looked Eileen over with a calculating eye, and when they were alone he said, "Brother, you sure know how to pick 'em! But you'd better watch out for that pretty filly, and don't give her any encouragement, or you'll have a problem on your hands."

"Don't worry," Brett said. "We're so busy here that I hardly know she's around."

"Well, she sure knows *you're* around. Brett, you've never looked at another gal since you first saw Jane—but that doesn't keep them from looking at you. Eileen may fool you, and she may even try to kid herself, but that girl would turn handsprings if you ever so much as crooked your little finger at her."

"Ben, you flatter me. But you've been living alone so long you've begun looking at the ladies with a roving eye. When are you going to take off in your Foolish Forties? Why don't *you* take her out on the town?"

"By golly, I'd like to," Ben said, "but I've got to catch the noon plane for Boston."

Ben's keen eyes had noticed what Brett had failed to observe: Eileen was magnetically attracted to Brett—so much that for the first few days she had become confused whenever their eyes met. Gradually she had overcome this as she realized that Brett had turned his mind off completely, as far as she was concerned. At first his total indifference to her as a woman was a relief to her. He addressed her as "Mrs. Emery," and gently corrected her one day when she said, "There's a long-distance call for you, Colonel Cable."

"I'm a civilian now," he said. "Let's forget the military title. It's too formal. By the way, I've noticed that everyone else in the office calls you by your first name. Would you prefer that I do, too?"

"Please do," she said casually, and for once she was able to keep from blushing when he looked at her.

Under the pressure of work, she soon grew accustomed to being in the same room with Brett and in close proximity to him. Gradually she learned to imitate his habit of avoiding anything other than a strictly business relationship, simply by ignoring her instinctive attraction to him and concentrating on the task of the moment. Sometimes she wondered if he could feel the same emanations that occasionally made her heart beat faster in spite of herself, but if so, he gave no sign of it, other than his brief, startled expression the first time he had looked up at her on that day when they had met. Like most former newspapermen, Brett had learned to concentrate all his faculties on the job at hand, oblivious to anyone around him. Occasionally, when he was working on a speech or a report and she was sure he was oblivious to anything else, she would study him furtively as she pretended to adjust her typewriter, with an expression that combined admiration and perplexity with a touch of exasperation.

As he became immersed in the duties of his complex assignment, Brett gradually became aware that there were factors affecting it which were unique even in his extensive public relations experience. He was accustomed to the open and obvious competition of business rivals for publicity in the news columns. Now he noticed a different type of competition in the form of news items having a subtly adverse effect on military morale and public opinion of the armed services—despite the best efforts of Secretary Wells to generate morale-building publicity. Even some of the Secretary's own statements were frequently reported in such a manner that undue emphasis was given to the derogatory aspects rather than to the constructive portions.

Colonel Howe pointed this out to Brett, and asked what could be done about it.

"Not much, I'm afraid," Brett said. "As long as there aren't any direct misquotations or actual distortions, we can't object to the way the headlines are written or how our releases are edited."

Delving further into this situation, Brett soon learned that it was by no means confined to the newspapers: other media apparently were being utilized to portray military service in anything but a favorable light. Matt Howe brought in a typical example: on the same day that one magazine published an article Brett had written for the Secretary's by-line, another large weekly magazine used full-page newspaper advertisements to announce its cover feature article, entitled "Why I'm Resigning from the Air Force."

"Can't we at least stop this sort of thing?" Matt asked.

"Not unless the fellow who wrote it is still in uniform. We've got no authority over civilians."

"I've already checked on that. The little stinker's already been separated."

"Let me see that article," Brett said. "Just as I thought. He didn't even write it. It's one of those staff-written things, by an anonymous 'ex-Colonel,'—'as told to' one of their stringers. Yes, here he is, right on their masthead. The fellow who really wrote it is one of their 'editorial associates'—which means he's on their payroll and writes under their direction."

"Yes, but that's one of the oldest and most respected family magazines in this country. Surely they wouldn't *knowingly* run down one of their own Armed Services!"

"There it is," Brett said. "You know it's bad for us, I know it's bad, and if they don't know it's bad—well, they just can't be that stupid."

"You mean you think they're actually doing this sort of thing *purposely?*"

"I'm not sure," Brett said, "but I'm going to find out. When will Secretary Wells be back?"

"He's on an extended inspection trip with Undersecretary Hale. They'll be gone two more weeks."

"That should be time enough. I'm all caught up on speech assignments. That'll give me time to do a bit of research."

"Let me know what you find out," Matt said, "and yell if you need any help. We've got to lick this thing—before it licks us."

"There's only one way to lick it, Matt, and that's to get the goods on whoever is doing it, with evidence no one can dispute. Otherwise we'd be way out on a thin, dry limb."

"You've already got a good start, right there in that magazine," Matt said, snorting.

"Nothing we could ever prove. We've got to find something that will stand up in court."

"That may be pretty hard to do."

"I know," Brett said, "but the stakes are worth it."

"They sure are. Good luck to you, Brett, and keep me posted on any new developments."

CHAPTER SIX

The Combat Art Exhibits

During the first two weeks of his new assignment, Brett saw very little of the rest of the Pentagon other than his own office and the Office of Public Relations, two floors below him by way of the stair-well next to his door.

When his first bi-weekly pay check was delivered, he walked around to the other side of the Pentagon to open an account in the branch office of a local bank. His route took him through the most heavily traveled corridor, on the inner or "A"-ring of the third floor. The walls of this corridor were lined with framed enlargements of photographs of combat scenes.

As he walked along the corridor, Brett glanced casually at these photographs, which he did not recall having seen during his previous tour of duty in the Pentagon. He noticed that many showed wounded American soldiers, while others showed them either dead or obviously dying. As he hurried along towards the bank, he could see that a considerable portion of these photographs conveyed an impression that would be distasteful even to anyone accustomed to seeing his fellow-men killed on the battlefield.

After opening an account and depositing his pay check, Brett walked all the way around the corridor where the pictures were hung, taking notes as he went along. Half-way around the corridor, he came to a plaque on the wall bearing a printed inscription:

THE U.S. ARMY IN ACTION

> The photographs in this corridor are part of the U.S. Army's Combat Photo Collection showing American personnel in action during World War II and the Korean War. Catalogs of this collection can be obtained through the Curator, Room 5 E 900.

Continuing, Brett checked each photograph as he walked along. Suddenly he came to a group of four paintings depicting personnel in uniforms that were obviously not American. One of these paintings showed gaunt soldiers staggering across a frozen landscape past a row of empty steel helmets hanging from rifles whose bayonets were stuck in the snow. The caption on this painting was "German Graves Along the Road to Stalingrad." Another painting showed burnt-out German tanks and abandoned equipment on a corpse-littered field, with all of the bodies in German uniforms. The other two paintings showed victorious Soviet troops wearing the Red Star insignia, herding German soldiers into barbed-wire pens. These were the only paintings among all the photographs.

Brett began to note the captions more closely. One huge picture showed three grinning men enthusiastically loading a large field artillery piece in a sandbagged gun emplacement which was littered with empty shell casings. A printed caption under the photograph stated: "The Fortunes of War: Two minutes after this scene was photographed, this gun and these men were obliterated by an enemy shell."

Another caption was headed *Tears of Compassion.* The photograph showed three soldiers seated on a rocky hillside. One soldier had his arms around another who was weeping, while the third sat nonchalantly smoking a cigarette and writing on a notepad behind them. The sub-caption stated: "A G.I. whose best friend has just been killed weeps unconsolably in the arms of a buddy, while behind them a medical corpsman methodically checks the dead man's dog-tags."

After completing his circuit of the "A" corridor, Brett walked upstairs to Room 5 E 900, where a sign by the door stated: "Curator of Combat Art." Brett knocked on the door and entered. There was a small, pasty-faced man seated behind a desk.

"Can I help you?" he asked Brett.

"Are you the Curator?" Brett asked.

"I am. What can I do for you?"

"That's quite an art collection you've got down on the third floor," Brett said. "Could I purchase one of your catalogs?"

"Thank you. The catalogs are free. How many would you like?"

"I'll only need one, thank you. Are there any other collections like that in the Pentagon?"

"Yes, but they're not as extensive as ours. The Air Force has some very dramatic photos in corridor 4-E, next to their Secretary's office, and there's a small collection of combat paintings down in the Pentagon Dispensary on the concourse."

"Thanks for the information," Brett replied.

"Not at all," the little man said. "Glad to help you."

Brett went first to corridor 4-E, taking notes as he inspected the Air Force photographs. He was not surprised to find that nearly half of the pictures showed U.S. planes being shot down, while only a few showed enemy planes being destroyed. There were several photographs showing dead or wounded American personnel, but Brett searched in vain for photographs of enemy casualties.

Even this did not prepare Brett for what he found when he strolled through the Pentagon Dispensary to look at the paintings on the walls. These paintings were particularly gruesome. Virtually all of them showed wounded American personnel in various stages of shock or agony, suffering from scabrous tropical skin diseases, or undergoing emergency surgery in primitive battlefield dressing-stations.

Brett returned to his office, summarized his notes, and went in to see Colonel Howe.

"Matt," Brett said, "did you ever take a good look at any of the combat art on display in this building?"

"Oh, I've seen the stuff around, but I don't pay much attention to it. Why?"

"What would you say its purpose is supposed to be?"

"Oh, it's probably just a way each of the services tries to show how it won the war, I suppose. Inter-service rivalry, I guess you'd call it. The Army's been strong for that sort of thing ever since their Air Corps became a separate Air Force."

"Sort of a way of putting their best foot forward, would you say?"

"That's about it, Brett. But they're always changing it around."

"Matt, which corridor here in the Pentagon is used the

most—by people on their way to lunch, to the bank, and down to the concourse?"

"I'd say the A-ring on the third floor, where they have to go to get to the cafeterias, to the bank, to pay their utility bills, and so on. Why?"

"Because that's where you'll find the biggest collection of anti-morale pictures in the Pentagon," Brett said. "Come along with me, and I'll give you the grand tour."

Matt could hardly believe his eyes as Brett showed him the Army Combat Art Collection. Brett started with the explanatory plaque, saying, "Remember, this is supposed to be a collection of *photographs,* showing American personnel in action. Now take a look at these paintings showing what happens to anyone who dares to attack our great Soviet allies."

"Well, I'll be . . ." Matt said, staring at the captions. "Right here in the Pentagon—under our very noses!"

"You haven't seen anything yet," Brett said. "Now, when officers assigned to the Pentagon suddenly get sent overseas, what's the last stop on their checkout list?"

"The Dispensary, for inoculations and a physical checkup."

"Right. Wait until you see *their* art collection. And when we get there, I want you to indicate which pictures you like—from the standpoint of inspiring you for an overseas assignment—and which ones rub you the wrong way."

There were 33 paintings on the corridor walls of the Dispensary, and Colonel Howe had violent reactions against all but two. "Why, that's the worst bunch of junk I ever saw!" he said. "And just look at it! Most of these aren't even good paintings!"

"Now let me show you the Air Force collection," Brett said.

"Oh, no! Don't tell me my own outfit's been sucked in, too!"

"They've got plenty of company," Brett said. "Come on."

By Matt's count, 42 per cent of the photographs in the Air Force collection showed his own side taking a beating, with only ten per cent of the pictures showing the enemy's planes being hit.

"Cheer up, Matt," Brett said. "Here are the figures on the Army's collection: U.S. dead or wounded, 11 per cent; enemy, *none*. Photographs favorable to our side, 35 per cent; those favorable to the enemy, 45 per cent. The remainder, which are neutral, just take up wall space which could be used to create a favorable impression."

"The Air Force ought to know better," Matt said. "I'll get on this right away."

"Wait a bit. You couldn't prove a thing. You'll have to admit these photos are dramatic. Maybe someone just wanted to show how tough the opposition was—and it really *was* tough. You were shot down, weren't you?"

"Yes, but we shot down a hell of a lot more of the enemy—almost every plane they had, before they gave up and yelled for mercy. And *we* won the war, as I recall."

"Not yet, we haven't," Brett said, laconically. "Incidentally, you'll notice that only two of the services are represented in these displays—the Army and the Air Force."

"Say, you're right! How about the Navy and the Marines? They must have a collection of pictures around somewhere."

"They probably do. Let me check and see how it compares with these, before you say anything that might alert whoever's doing this sort of thing either purposely or unintentionally."

"Good idea," Matt said. "The more ammunition we can get, the better."

Brett walked back to the E-ring and went down to the Office of Public Relations, where he stopped at the desk of Major Joe Tuttle.

"Hello, Brett," Tuttle said. "What's new? You haven't brought any speeches in for clearance lately."

"Secretary Wells is out of town, Tutt. By the way, I've noticed that the Army and the Air Force have combat art displays in the Pentagon. How about our own outfit, and the Navy? Don't we have a pretty good story to tell, pictorially?"

"You bet we do, and we're telling it. But we're one jump ahead of the others; ours is mechanized. Haven't you heard about our Operation Paint-Brush?"

"No. I've been away for a couple of years, you know. Please educate me."

"Well, we've got the finest combat art collection there is. And it's on the road, going around from city to city—two trucks loaded with one hundred paintings by well-known magazine illustrators who served with the Marines and the Navy. When we had it here in the Pentagon, down on the Concourse, over fifty thousand people stopped by to see it, by actual count. You really ought to see it."

"I'd like to," Brett said. "Where is it?"

"It's in Cleveland just now, on a tour of Mid-Western cities, but it's scheduled for Baltimore next month, and you can drive up there in an hour."

"Who runs it, Tutt?"

"Some outfit connected with Navy Archives in the old Navy Building over on Constitution Avenue," Tuttle said, consulting a directory. "Here it is: Combat Art Section, Navy Archives, Room 9020, Old Navy Building."

"Who do they report to?"

"Navy Public Relations."

"Why aren't they in the Pentagon then?"

"They need a lot of space to store all their paintings. They've got thousands of 'em, going all the way back to the Civil War."

"Sounds like a pretty big operation."

"Oh, not so big; only about three people run it. A couple of Lieutenants on temporary active duty, who are on loan from one of the big metropolitan art museums, with a civilian gal in charge. All of the services have dozens of little outfits like that, tucked around in various buildings all over Washington, to beat the budget-trimmers."

"How do the Public Relations people manage to keep track of it all?" Brett asked.

"They don't. If it weren't for a few dedicated Civil Service people, like the gal in charge of the combat art, there'd be no continuity. It's the civilian personnel that really keep things running, year after year, with little or no recognition. I doubt if anyone from Pub Rel has called on her in months."

"I think I'll drop in and pay her a visit," Brett said. "I'd like to see the rest of her art collection."

"You'll never get past her office. She'll hang onto you like a leech, trying to get more money for her operation, and she guards those pictures of hers like she'd painted them herself. No one who calls on her ever goes back twice, after she pours all her woes into his ear for a couple of hours."

Brett found Major Tuttle's description accurate. There was a middle-aged woman in a dingy office, and the moment he introduced himself she asked him to help her put pressure on the Secretary of the Navy for more operating funds.

"I'm afraid I can't help you with that," Brett said. "I wanted to get a catalog of the paintings on tour with your Operation Paint-Brush."

"Ah'm very sorry," she said, with an affected Bostonian accent, "but we've nevah had enough funds to issue a catalog. Furthahmore, we rotate the paintings frequently, to give them wideh circulation."

"Do you mind if I look at some of those you have in storage?"

"Ah'm so sorry, but it's agaynst owah rules. You see, it takes two men to lift each painting off the shelves without hahming it, and we'd be chahged ovahtime for their labah."

"If we provided you with a squad of Marines, could you select one hundred paintings suitable for display in the Pentagon along the walls adjacent to the Secretary of the Navy's offices, and supervise their installation?" Brett asked casually.

"Of coahse. How simply wondehful! When could we staht?"

"Right away. I'll arrange for the men and a truck, and we'll take good care of your paintings. Just let me know when they'll arrive, and I'll ask Public Relations to prepare a press release."

"Oh, thank you *so* much!" she gushed. "You're just a dahling!"

Returning to the Pentagon, Brett told Colonel Howe what had transpired, adding, "I want to see just what kind of a collection she brings over, and how it compares with the other exhibits."

"Good idea, Brett. Let me know when the paintings arrive, and we'll look at them together."

The next day the Corporal in charge of the Marines in the work detail telephoned Brett that the paintings had been installed "according to the instructions of the lady in charge."

"Wait there," Brett said. He called Colonel Howe, and they inspected the paintings. As they anticipated, many of the paintings showed bloody U.S. casualties, American planes in flames, U.S. Navy ships exploding, weeping Marines, and disfiguring wounds.

"Take these back where they came from," Brett said. "Colonel Howe and I will meet you there."

Over the shrill protests of the woman in charge of the Combat Art Section, the two men walked into the rooms where the paintings were stored, accompanied by the squad of Marines. They found hundreds of magnificent combat paintings hidden away in a dusty room, which was unlocked for them only after Colonel Howe told the Corporal to kick the door open. After selecting paintings which showed American personnel in a favorable light, Brett personally supervised their installation, in a well-balanced display representing all branches of the Navy and the Marine Corps. Instead of two paintings showing U.S. Navy ships exploding under suicidal enemy attacks, which he had removed from each side of the Secretary of the Navy's office, Brett hung two which showed enemy aircraft carriers being sunk by U.S. Navy planes.

Two days later, the Navy's Director of Public Relations

was somewhat mystified to receive a personal letter of appreciation from the Secretary of the Navy in acknowledgment of a much-needed improvement reflecting great credit on the Navy Department. Colonel Howe gave Brett an information copy of the letter, adding that he had sent copies to the Secretaries of the Army and the Air Force, with the suggestion that they compare their own exhibits with that of the Navy Department.

A few days later, to Colonel Howe's vast satisfaction, the Army and the Air Force overhauled their exhibits, eliminating all pictures of their own men being killed or wounded, and substituting photographs showing the enemy on the run.

Matt Howe chortled as the offending pictures were replaced. "You've got a good eye, Brett," he said. "I've been walking by those damned depressing pictures for nearly a year without noticing anything unusual about them."

"It's the overall effect that counts, Matt. Very few people stop to look at each picture individually. If the net impact of the whole display conveys an impression of enemy strength and our weakness, whom does it benefit the most?"

"Certainly not our side," Matt said. "Come to think of it, when I was a P.O.W. in Germany during the last few weeks of the war, all they gave us to read were books and magazines filled with pictures showing the Germans kicking hell out of the Poles, the French, and the Russians. But I can't recall even one photo of a German plane being shot down or a German casualty. No wonder they swallowed all that guff about being the Master Race. If they read enough of it, they probably thought they were invincible."

"That works both ways," Brett said. "As one great soldier wrote, 'in war the psychological factors are often decisive. An adversary who feels inferior is in reality so.' "

"Who said that? He couldn't be more right."

"Marshal Mannerheim of Finland."

"One of the greatest," Matt said. "He beat the Soviets twice."

"Yes, but how many people know that? Most people know only Molotov's version, which was given much wider circulation."

"I see what you mean, Brett. We've got to keep telling our own story, and telling it right, because if we don't, the other side will tell it for us—and they'll tell it their way."

"That's about it," Brett said, "and now I've got to get back to work on that survey. As the sign on the sun-dial says, it's much later than we think."

CHAPTER SEVEN

The Philadelphia Pageant

Before departing on his extended inspection trip, Secretary Wells had instructed Colonel Howe to expedite Brett's security clearance. Ordinarily, several months were required to investigate the background of civilian employees in the super-grade category, but Brett's previous military service, involving security clearances necessary for him to have access to extremely sensitive information including battle plans, enabled the Military Intelligence Division of the Department of Defense to issue his security clearance within two weeks after he had been sworn in as a Special Assistant to Wells.

"M.I.D. has given you a clean bill of health," Colonel Howe had informed Brett. "Now you can sit in for Mr. Wells on some of these long-winded inter-service conferences that take up so much of his time."

Shortly after the combat art episode, Matt Howe asked Brett to represent Wells at a luncheon conference in the office of the Deputy Secretary of Defense.

"It's something about a moral rejuvenation movement," Matt said. "Some religious organization is involved, which puts it in the public relations field."

Brett attended the conference, where he listened to a long, rambling talk by an impressive-looking man in clerical garb who was introduced as the Reverend Dr. Bottsworth, Chairman of the Civilian Council of Churches. Representatives of all of the armed services were present, including the senior military chaplain of each service.

"The Church Militant can revitalize the nation's defense," Dr. Bottsworth declared, "and the CCC can strengthen the moral authority of the Armed Forces Chaplains." He then outlined a nebulous program for providing moral guidance to teen-age draftees, including a grandiose plan for a National CCC Conference. This was to be staged in Philadelphia with an opening ceremony in front of the Liberty Bell, as the beginning of a nationwide Pastor-Chaplain movement to carry out his program.

Brett took notes as Dr. Bottsworth talked, and grew uneasy as the vague, unrealistic proposal was described. When the meeting had ended, Brett sought out the Chaplain General, who had sat with his arms folded when the others had applauded the proposal.

"Padre," Brett said, "I notice you didn't seem too enthusiastic about that proposal we just heard."

The Chaplain General snorted. "Proposal! That was just a lot of double-talk, and the others fell for it. Bottsworth's an old hand at that sort of thing. That's why he by-passed my office: he knows we're onto him."

"You've known him before, then?"

"You bet I have—too well. He's a renegade ex-chaplain who resigned during the middle of the war and tried to take over another chaplain's church. Almost got away with it, too. But the congregation finally got wise to him and then he organized a bunch of screwball ministers into this CCC thing. It's a notorious outfit of self-seeking misfits, and most of its top echelon are shameless charlatans.

Bottsworth's the worst of the bunch. He's always using political influence to give us the run-around. Now he's sold SecDef's Deputy on this phony program, which is far beyond our manpower capabilities; we keep only a skeleton organization in peace-time. This thing will bog us down completely, and it'll require heavy financial support—much more than our budget can stand."

"Bottsworth indicated that he could get plenty of financial assistance from civic organizations."

"Don't you believe it. That's why he was in here playing both ends against the middle. Once he gets Pentagon backing he'll use it as a club to raise the funds, and Uncle Sam will have to foot the bill. Wait until our next meeting on this; you'll see."

"Thanks for the fill-in, *Padre*. I had a feeling something was wrong when I couldn't make any sense out of the notes I was taking."

"That's the way he operates. He can talk for an hour, and when you try to boil down what he said, it all evaporates into thin air."

"Why can't we back out before it's too late?"

"I'm afraid we're already hooked. Look at this. Here's an advance copy of the CCC Newsletter."

Brett stared at the article, which was illustrated with a photograph of the Secretary of Defense. "Good grief!" he said. "We've already endorsed it. What a way to operate!"

The Chaplain General smiled ruefully. "That's not all," he said. "Look at their financial statement. They're not only broke, but in debt several thousand dollars."

Brett scanned the financial statement. "H'mm," he said, "this is interesting. They owe two thousand dollars to somebody they commissioned to write a script called

'America the Beautiful—a Pageant of Brotherly Love,' to be performed by a tremendous cast of church members and members of the Armed Services, under the direction of the author, Michael Irwin. Now, I wonder who could be such a sucker as that, to write for this bunch on speculation?"

"He probably fell for Bottsworth's line, just like the others. This pageant is the come-on. It's to be filmed for nationwide distribution, as the basis for 'a national Pastor-Chaplain program for the moral indoctrination of all teen-age draftees.' What a lot of rot!"

Brett frowned slightly as he studied the newsletter. "That's a mighty ambitious program, *Padre*. Let's get together again after your next meeting with this outfit."

"Good. I'll keep my eye on them. They're a bunch of mighty slick operators. Just to show you how fast they move, they've set up a meeting tomorrow morning with a CCC planning committee, and I've already been told that we're to co-operate with them fully. I'd appreciate it if you'd sit in with us, because I'm almost alone in my opposition to Bottsworth and all his works, and he's told the other chaplains it's only professional jealousy on my part. The meeting's in my office at ten o'clock. Can you come?"

"I'll be glad to. This doesn't look like something I'd ask Secretary Wells to endorse."

The CCC planning committee consisted of three chaplains from the Philadelphia area. One wore the uniform of a Navy Captain with the gold cross insignia, and the others were Colonels in the Army and the Air Force. The Captain was the chairman of the committee. He appeared very sure of himself.

"We have some great news, gentlemen," he said. "The

White House has given its official blessing to our project, and the Vice President himself will officiate at the opening ceremonies. This will be a memorable occasion indeed." He held up a leather-bound folder. "I'm also happy to announce that the pageant script has been completed, and it's simply magnificent. I'm absolutely sure that there'll be a full-length movie of it produced by a major Hollywood studio, in addition to the television version. In fact, I can tell you—confidentially—that the author has already received assurance to that effect. He's a real professional, and has many Hollywood contacts."

The Chaplain General looked skeptical. "Has the author been paid yet?" he asked bluntly.

The Captain smiled patronizingly. "Better than that, General," he said. "Mr. Irwin has such faith in the success of our project that he has not even submitted a bill for his services, and has agreed to accept payment later from the motion picture royalties after the pageant is filmed."

"What's his percentage of the take?" the Chaplain General asked.

"That will be spelled out in due time, when the contract is signed," the Captain said. "But meanwhile the important thing is that the completed script has not only been delivered and approved, but rehearsals have already been started under the direction of the author, Michael Irwin."

"Who approved the script?" the Chaplain General asked.

"The Chairman of the CCC, Dr. Bottsworth himself," the Captain replied. "As I told you, the White House has given him a green light, and we're going ahead at full speed."

"Do you have an extra copy of the script?" Brett asked.

"Not with me," the Captain said. "This is the original, which will be delivered to the White House."

"May I glance through it?" Brett asked.

"Certainly," the Captain said, handing Brett the leather-bound folder.

Brett glanced through the pages, which were electrically typed in a script that resembled printing. It was clearly an expensive reproduction.

"This is a beautiful piece of work," Brett said. "I wish I had a copy to accompany my recommendation to Secretary Wells. He could be of great assistance to you in anything affecting military morale—which your project obviously does."

One of the visiting chaplains looked up brightly. "I have one of the rehearsal copies," he said eagerly. "Of course it isn't bound as nicely as that one, but I'm sure you could get a proper folder for it." He opened a briefcase, took out a thick manila envelope, and handed it to Brett.

The Captain glared. "You know we can't do that, Colonel," he said sharply. "That copy is for the Deputy Secretary of Defense."

The Chaplain General smiled. "That's no problem," he said. "We have a photo-duplication setup that can copy the whole thing in an hour. I'll run off a couple of copies—one for Secretary Wells and another for our office. We'll have it on Deputy SecDef's desk before he's back from lunch."

The Captain hesitated, and Brett handed the envelope to the Chaplain General.

"Very well," the Captain said, "but I must warn you that this material is copyrighted, and no publicity whatever regarding it may be released without the written permission of the author."

"The author?" Brett repeated.

"Yes. He holds the copyright. Premature release of the script could jeopardize his negotiations with Hollywood."

"Don't worry," the Chaplain General said. "It'll be in safe hands here in the Pentagon."

After the CCC committee had departed, the Chaplain General asked Brett, "Well, what do you think they're up to?"

"I don't like the smell of it," Brett said. "No writer worth his salt would take on such an assignment without a substantial advance or a signed contract, unless he was a big-name author who could afford to donate his services for the prestige—and I've never heard of this fellow Michael Irwin. His script looks like the work of a professional playwright, from the little I saw of it. And he'd have to know something about the stage, to direct a pageant of this size. But he's in this thing too deep, if it's copyrighted in his name—which gives him control of the purse-strings. If his script sells to the movies, for a film to be made with the assistance of the Department of Defense, the royalties could be tremendous."

"You mean someone's getting a kick-back—Bottsworth, for example?"

"Maybe. But it might even go beyond that. That Captain didn't want us to see the script, which doesn't make sense when they've already distributed several hundred copies to the people who are rehearsing it. And he used pretty strong language when he *warned* you not to publicize it without the author's written permission. After all, the Armed Services are involved, and as the direct representative of the Secretary of Defense in the religious field, you're considerably senior to anyone in their organization."

"Remember, I've been by-passed in this from the beginning, through high-level political pressure all the way up to the White House. But that's the way they always operate. What do you think their game is?"

"I don't know," Brett said. "Maybe we can get a better idea after we study that script."

"Good. I'll let you know as soon as it's duplicated."

An hour later, the Chaplain General telephoned Brett, "The first copy is ready," he said. "I've been reading some of it as it came off the machine. It's absolute gibberish. Can you come over?"

A few minutes later, Brett and the Chaplain General were scanning the pageant script.

"What a travesty!" the Chaplain General said. " 'America the Beautiful'—and it reads like a nightmare in a mad-house. Here, take a look at this page of drivel."

Brett jotted notes on a pad as he studied the script. After he had finished reading it he glanced at his notes. "Quite a job," he said. "Do you see the pattern, *Padre?*"

The Chaplain General looked puzzled. "You mean you can make order out of all this chaotic drivel?" he said. "All I see is a bunch of violent mob scenes, juvenile delinquency, terrorized parents, crime and corruption. What on earth does all this have to do with providing moral guidance to teen-age draftees?"

"Not a thing. That's what makes it so significant—the omissions, as well as the emphasis on a few recurring themes. Three scenes involve intimidation of students or teachers by hoodlums armed with switch-blade knives. The parents are depicted as stupid, the teachers are incompetent and the police are corrupt. The heroes are the juvenile delinquents who rebel against all forms of restraint. In the war scenes the non-coms are brutal and the officers are yellow. The only ones killed are those foolish enough to stand up against overwhelming odds. Five passages emphasize the futility of war, and four repeat the I'm-too-young-to-die theme. One whole scene is devoted to the dying agonies of a young soldier who slowly bleeds to death in the center of the stage, surrounded by heartless medics, while his buddies weep, or scream at the stupidity of the high brass. Religion is a farce, wars are started by profiteering aircraft companies, and depressions are inevitable. The world's only hope is to ban all further tests of atomic weapons—that's in there four times. Nothing in the script is *constructive*."

The Chaplain General leafed through the script again, and his face grew grim. "By Judas, you're right!" he said. "I knew it rubbed me the wrong way, but it's such a hodge-podge of irrelevant scenes, with all those people marching on and off stage, that I missed the overall effect of the thing."

"That's just what the author intended. He's covered his tracks pretty well, until you take his script apart theme by theme and add up the totals."

"What would you say it all adds up to?"

"I wouldn't say just yet. Too many important people already have endorsed this project. You and I are prejudiced, because we know Bottsworth's background. What we need now is to get an objective evaluation of this script from an impartial, authoritative source, and then to get a line on the author—find out what makes him tick and who he really works for."

"Which comes first?"

"The script," Brett said. "If you'll handle that, I'll

check the author's pedigree with Military Intelligence."

"Where should I take it? I'm naive about this sort of thing."

"Just send it up to DSI—the Division of Special Investigations," Brett said, removing the title page with the author's name. "They're the experts on cryptanalysis who can separate code messages from innocent-looking letters. Ask them if it has any special meaning, and they'll take it apart line by line."

Brett picked up the telephone and called Gib Morrison, who was now convalescing at home. "Gib," he said, "who should I talk to in MID to get a line on someone who might possibly be active in the re-enlistment area we talked about?"

"On whose side?" Gib asked. "Ours or theirs?"

"Theirs."

"Termites, eh?"

"Possibly. We're double-checking. But we can't get a fix on one character."

"That's simple, Brett. Just ask MID for a name-check, and if there's anything shady in his background it'll show up."

"Who handles that area?"

"Mead Jayson, a civilian specialist. He's a GS-15, and he knows his business."

"Thanks a lot, Gib."

"Not at all. How are you coming along?"

"I'm slowly getting educated."

"Good. Let me know if I can help in any way."

At the MID reception desk Brett identified himself, and an MP escorted him to Mead Jayson's office. Jayson was a slight, thin-faced man in his early fifties, with a solemn expression and steel-rimmed glasses that gave him a scholarly appearance.

"Colonel Morrison suggested that I see you," Brett said. "I'd like to get a routine check on a writer named Michael Irwin, whose work is under consideration for a project involving the endorsement of the Department of Defense."

"Is there anything suspicious in his background?" Jayson asked.

"No, but the project is important, and we can't find anything about this fellow's background."

"That shouldn't take long," Jayson said. "The Government Security Bureau can give us the answer in a few minutes." He pressed a button on his telephone and told his secretary, "Please get me Merle Dawson at the GBS. He should be there by now."

"Dawson's the GBS liaison officer assigned to the Pentagon," he explained to Brett. "He just left here half an hour ago." After a short pause his telephone rang, and he picked up the receiver. "Hello, Merle? You made a quick trip. Here's a name-check request. Michael Irwin, I-R-W-I-N, no middle initial. He's a writer. No other information. Shall I hold on?" He nodded to Brett, and sat silently waiting for a reply. After a few minutes he said, "Yes, Merle. No information? Thanks a lot. I'll see you tomorrow."

He turned to Brett and said, "There's no record of him in the GBS alphabetical files, which means there are no derogatory reports on him from a security standpoint. We can run credit and reference checks if you like."

"That won't be necessary. We know his credit's good with some rather prominent people who have endorsed him and approved his work. Thank you for your trouble."

"No trouble at all. Please call on us at any time. It's always better to be sure than sorry."

Late that afternoon the Chaplain General telephoned Brett and said, "I've got a report from DSI on the pageant script."

"Already? They moved fast on that one," Brett said. "What's the verdict—good or bad?"

"Well, it's a lot like your summary, only in much greater detail. They really went through it with a fine-toothed comb. But their evaluation is short and to the point. Here, I'll read it to you: 'This script is a masterpiece of subtly subversive literature, designed to indoctrinate both the audience and the participating cast in the tolerance and acceptance of totalitarian ideology, without exposing either the author or the producers to charges which would stand up if defended on the grounds of freedom of speech and expression.' In other words, they say it's even worse than we thought it was—and then tell us there's nothing we can do to stop it."

"We're not licked yet," Brett said, "but we've got to move carefully. We may not know *who* Michael Irwin is, but at least we know that he's no amateur. That makes it much harder for him to cover his tracks; all professional writers have individual peculiarities of style, and I've yet to meet one without pride of authorship. He's obviously using a *nom-de-plume,* but it shouldn't be too hard to smoke him out."

CHAPTER EIGHT

"Freedom of the Press"

The next morning as he scanned the Washington newspapers, Brett saw a news item about the Pastor-Chaplain Program of the Civilian Council of Churches. The story carried a Philadelphia date-line, and quoted enthusiastic comments by the Chairman of the city's Civic Affairs Committee.

Brett clipped the item and showed it to Colonel Howe. "Matt," he said, "here's something that's getting out of hand. I've prepared an interim report on that assignment you gave me yesterday. This isn't completed staff work, or anywhere near it—but I'd like some guidance on how to proceed at this point."

Matt studied the clipping and the preliminary report attached to it. "This is pretty sticky, Brett," he said. "Looks like a stage version of that combat art operation. And this directly involves military morale and public opinion of the Armed Forces—which puts our boss on the spot."

"Right—and while he's out of the country."

"We'd better refer this up the line. We report to Undersecretary Hale—and he's with Mr. Wells."

"Who's acting for Hale in his absence?"

"Fred Gruber, his senior Special Assistant. He's a GS-

18—the top Civil Service super-grade. You'd better take this on up to him—not your report, which Mr. Wells must see first; just review the facts briefly, and give Gruber the script with DSI's evaluation. He'll probably pass it right up to the next echelon, as soon as he hears about the White House angle. This is *really* a hot potato!"

Fred Gruber was a stocky, unsmiling man about Brett's age, with iron-gray hair and thick-lensed glasses. He listened without changing expression while Brett outlined the situation, then glanced at the report attached to the script.

"Thank you, Mr. Cable," he said. "I've already heard about this program. I'll look into it further and recommend appropriate action for the Undersecretary to take on his return."

Brett waited for a moment, and there was an awkward pause. Gruber looked at him for several seconds, then asked, "Is there anything else you wish to discuss, Mr. Cable?"

"Yes, there is," Brett said quietly. "The organization involved in this project has a shady background and a shaky financial status, and as that clipping indicates, they've got no compunctions about using anyone—civilian or military—to promote this project. Don't you think someone ought to suggest to the Philadelphia Civic Affairs Committee that they check further into the background of this self-styled religious organization before endorsing it to the public?"

"I wouldn't worry about that if I were you, Mr. Cable. Undersecretary Hale happens to be a close friend of the Governor of Pennsylvania. Mr. Hale will take appropriate action, I can assure you. Just leave this with me, and

I'll keep you informed on any developments. Thank you for coming in, Mr. Cable," he said, curtly concluding the discussion.

Brett returned to his office, where Matt Howe was waiting for him.

"How did it go?" Matt asked.

"Gruber didn't seem very concerned," Brett said. "He's going to sit on it until Undersecretary Hale returns, I'm afraid."

"Well, at least it's out of our hair until then. And we've got plenty to do without getting tangled up in that sort of thing. Here's another job for you that just came in. It's a writing assignment—an article for Mr. Wells to sign. The editor of *Our Armed Forces* wants an article on the problems of military morale, and we always cooperate with them, even though it's not an official publication. Here's the request, forwarded by OPR with a strong endorsement recommending approval," Matt said, handing Brett a manila folder.

Brett read the endorsement, which was signed by the Director of Public Relations of the Department of Defense. "That's a pretty strong endorsement of an unofficial magazine," he commented. "Where can I get a copy?"

"I'll have OPR send you a half-dozen back issues from their files," Matt said. "They usually get advance copies of all the magazines."

After Matt left, Brett handed the forwarding endorsement to Eileen. "Please make me a copy of this," he said, "and file it away for future reference. Too many people seem much more interested in our problems than in our accomplishments."

When the magazines arrived, Brett picked up the latest issue. On the cover was an official Air Force photograph of a blazing jet fighter with the pilot trapped in the cockpit. The lead article described "unnecessary" training accidents and demanded a Congressional investigation of the incompetence of the "high brass." Another article by an anonymous Army wife told why she did not want her husband to re-enlist. An announcement of a forthcoming feature promised to expose "the worst scandal in the history of the U.S. Navy—the true story of the sinking of the U.S.S. *Minneapolis*." An editorial recommended relaxing "brutal" military discipline and urged enlisted men to air their complaints in letters to the editor. Six pages of such letters were published, with sympathetic comments by the editor. Other features included "the ten best movies, books and magazine articles of the month," selected and recommended by the magazine's editor, Lionel Gundy.

Brett copied this list, then walked down to the vast Pentagon Concourse, a huge shopping center for the building's military and civilian workers. In the display window of the big bookshop, he found tall stacks of three of the "ten best books," and inside the store he found the other seven prominently displayed. All of these books were on military subjects, and each one criticized, depreciated or ridiculed one of the Armed services. Four of the books were novels in the "best-seller" class.

The Pentagon magazine stand—largest in the Washington area, in the center of the crowded concourse, had a special rack for copies of "Our Armed Forces." Next to it was an enormous display labeled "Magazines for Men." From this display, Brett purchased an armful of the magazines containing the recommended articles. He then walked through the big chain drug store, where he found an equally large display of the same magazines. Like the magazine stand display, the drug store's display was surrounded by young enlisted men in uniform, so that customers had to stand in line to buy copies.

Checking through the magazines he had purchased, Brett found that almost all of the recommended articles were even more anti-military than the books. All of these magazines were similar in format and layout. The cover illustrations showed military personnel in violent action, either wounded, fear-stricken, or fighting against hopeless odds. The articles and stories were illustrated with photographs or garish paintings showing fly-blown corpses, flaming aircraft, exploding ships, bloody wounds, violent death, and burials at sea. A large section of each magazine was devoted to photographs of nearly-nude models in suggestive poses. Each magazine contained several stories or articles bordering on obscenity, and articles on prostitution or the use of narcotics appeared in almost every issue. Checking further, Brett found that the majority of the objectionable magazines were published by a few large firms, with one publishing house—Dawn Publications—producing the most flagrantly anti-morale material.

On a hunch, Brett called Military Personnel and found that Lionel Gundy, the editor of *Our Armed Forces,* was a former Army sergeant with a bad-conduct discharge. Gundy had a long record of court-martial convictions, twice for being absent without leave while restricted to his base with a venereal disease. He had served on several service publication staffs, including the European edition of the Army's official newspaper.

Armed with this information, Brett took a copy of *Our Armed Forces* and its ten recommended magazines to Mead Jayson in the Military Intelligence Division. Jayson listened patiently while Brett outlined the situation and then sent for a thick file labeled "Battle Horror Publications." This file contained issues of some particularly gruesome ten-cent "comics" booklets and half a dozen different magazines—all published by Dawn Publications.

This file was stamped "SECRET." Jayson reviewed its contents. "These comics and magazines were sent in from Korea," he said, "where they were being distributed surreptitiously to the front-line troops of a regiment with an unusually high incidence of combat failures—men who couldn't pull a trigger or who broke and ran when confronted by the enemy. We sent the file to DSI for evaluation. They labeled it 'a sinister example of enemy psychological warfare aimed at undermining the morale of combat personnel.' Our forwarding endorsement agreed with the evaluation and recommended action to stop further publication and distribution of these publications. The action addressee is OPR/DD—the Office of Public Relations of the Department of Defense. They called in the publisher and business manager of Dawn Publications, who promised to clean up their magazines and comics. That was several years ago. You can see for yourself how little effect it's had. These fellows are not only still operating, but have quadrupled their output."

"You mean that no other action was taken?" Brett asked incredulously.

"Here's the last entry in the file, a memo from the Director of OPR/DD: 'Return to MID. No action is recommended in this case, since it involves the question of freedom of the press. It is recommended that this file be classified TOP SECRET to prevent disclosure of its contents to unauthorized persons—particularly representatives of the press.' That killed it. The case is now officially and permanently closed."

"But these are civilian publications," Brett said. "*Our Armed Forces* is almost a semi-official publication which is distributed through our canteens, post exchanges, and ships' stores. And people in uniform write for it—including officers."

Jayson lifted his hands in a gesture of helplessness. "Look, we've been through this thing time and again, and everyone who's tackled it has had his ears pinned back. Remember, Lionel Gundy is now a civilian, and is free to write as he pleases—so long as he doesn't break any laws. And no laws have been broken, according to the Pentagon's best legal minds. Please, for your own sake, don't forget that anything involving freedom of the press is a hot potato that has withered many a flowering government career."

"That's the second time I've heard that expression today," Brett said. "Our office seems to attract hot potatoes like a magnet."

"Your boss has his problems, all right. But this business is full of problems. Do you want me to add these magazines to our collection?"

"No, I'll hang onto them. At least they're not classified, like those in your file. Thanks for educating me. I'm going to start my own collection, and I think I know where to look next."

That evening at home, Brett looked into the magazines and comics that his children had been reading. Jimmy, his eight-year-old son, had a large stack of ten-cent comics. His daughter June, who was ten, had a shelf full of lurid film star and confession magazines. Jack, the eldest at twelve, had an extensive collection of twenty-five-cent men's magazines—far more than his weekly allowance would enable him to buy. All four groups of publications were heavily represented by Dawn Publications.

Brett was told that Jimmy had "traded" for his comics, June had borrowed hers from school-mates, and Jack had checked his out from the school library. Brett was inclined to doubt this last explanation, but Jack stoutly defended it, adding that his teacher "fought in the war as a commando and reads the war stories to us in class. And he teaches us judo at recess. He's killed men with his bare hands, and he's promised to show us how."

"You've got to return these magazines," Brett told his children. "I'll get you some better ones." He then drove to the neighborhood drug store to purchase some decent substitutes. There he found a smaller version of the same setup he had found in the Pentagon; magazines filled with violence, brutality, crime, and sexual promiscuity outnumbered the so-called "family" magazines more than ten to one. At the stationery store next to his children's school it was even worse: the magazine section was separated from the soda fountain by a plywood partition, where several children browsed undisturbed through stacks of gaudy-covered magazines and a vast assortment of comics.

Returning to his home, Brett examined his children's homework assignments and the textbooks they were using. June was studying a history book which portrayed the United States as a crassly capitalistic aggressor nation continually involved in wars of acquisition which it entered belatedly and won only with the support of its allies—especially the USSR in World War II. There was no mention of the Korean War, even though the book was labeled as a "revised edition—completely up to date."

The older boy, Jack, was writing a report, as part of his "Social Studies," on a book called "America the Beautiful" which described the "social revolution" in terms of the clash between labor and capital. There was much emphasis on the "Great Depression" which was attributed to the abuses of "Big Business." At the end of each chapter there was a question-and-answer section which embrazenly repeated the socialistic themes which were emphasized throughout the book.

Brett laid the books aside, deeply disturbed. Far into the night, he discussed the situation with his wife. Jane was shocked, and her first reaction was that they should protest to the school authorities. Then she grew fearful. "Maybe they're in on it, too," she said. "In that case they could cause trouble for the children—and for you in your job. Darling, I wish that we'd never got mixed up in this sort of thing. I don't like it. No one seems concerned about it but you, and you can't fight it alone."

"Someone's got to fight it," Brett said. "We're all in it now—even the children. I won't stand by and see them taken over like this. And you wouldn't want me to, either."

"No, I wouldn't. But please be careful. This thing is so big it frightens me."

"Don't worry, my love. I'm not going to do anything rash. But one thing for sure: I'm going to keep an eye on that school, and I'm going to have a good close look at Jack's teacher. Now that we know what's going on, it shouldn't be too hard to find out who's behind it, and why."

CHAPTER NINE

Progressive Education

That night Brett slept fitfully. At dawn he awoke, and when the alarm-clock aroused Jane half an hour later she found him reading through the children's textbooks as he lay beside her in their big double bed.

At breakfast he said, "Darling, has it ever occurred to you that our children can't read very well?"

"Yes, Brett, but remember that we've moved around a lot, and that they've been to several schools—including that poor excuse of a school in the tropics for two years."

"I know, but even with that, it seems to me that they're a good deal farther behind than we were at the same age—especially Jack. When I was his age I was reading several books a week, but I've never seen him look at anything except something he's told to 'look up'—which isn't even homework."

"He's never failed a grade, nor have any of the others."

"Yes, but we don't even know how they stand, with the grading system in use today. In my day we used a percentage system, with seventy-five the passing grade. Anyone who got marks below that failed, and had to make it up or take the course over. Today everyone seems to pass, and the grading system is so vague we never know how our children really are doing in their school work. Just look at these report cards. They don't even use grades any more: 'Jack is progressing satisfactorily at all levels, but his group co-operation could be improved.' That doesn't tell us a thing."

"I know. But at the P.T.A. meeting they explained that it's all part of the new 'progressive' education system, which they endorsed."

"Results are what count, and our children aren't progressing fast enough to suit me. Jack's the one I'm most worried about. His writing is a scrawl, he can't spell, and he uses bad grammar. The others are young enough to catch up, but soon he'll be in high school, and he's big for his age."

After breakfast Brett handed Jack a textbook and said, "Here, son, I want you to read a page of this aloud."

Jack took the book and started to read, slowly and haltingly, with many errors and substitutions. Words having more than three syllables either stopped him, or he skipped them completely.

Jane glanced at Brett with a worried look. "Let's try something easier," she said, handing the boy a child's reader.

Even the simpler words were beyond Jack's ability, and Brett realized that his son had merely been repeating his own version of fragments of words he could understand.

"Let's go back to the beginning," Brett said. "Jack, let's see if you remember your alphabet."

Jack looked puzzled, and Brett said, "Just recite your ABC's, son, the way you learned them."

Jack cleared his throat, raised his voice, and began to sing: "A,B,C,D,E,F,G . . ."

Brett interrupted. "You don't have to sing them. Just say them—just as we're talking here now."

Jack started over, in a conversational voice, but with the same rhythm: "A,B,C,D,E,F,G; H,I,J,K, Ella, Menno, P; Q,R,S . . ."

"Wait," Brett said. "Let's start all over."

Again Jack started, in a singsong voice, and repeated the same mistake: for the letters L, M, N, and O, he again said, "Ella, Menno."

Jane and Brett looked at each other. Brett handed Jack a pencil and a sheet of paper. "Here," he said, "let's try writing it down."

Jack wrote painfully, in awkward capital letters, until he passed the letter *K,* then paused doubtfully.

"Go ahead, son," Brett said, "write the rest of it—every letter you know."

Jack continued, starting with the letter *P,* until he reached the end of the alphabet. There were four letters missing: *L, M, N,* and *O*.

Brett and Jane stared silently at the sheet of paper.

Jack looked up at his parents with a troubled expression. "Have I done something wrong?" he asked.

Brett patted Jack's shoulder reassuringly. "No, son, you haven't done anything wrong. You're doing the best you can, and no one can do more. But you do need help with your reading, and we'll see that you get it. Now, run along to school, and keep on doing your best."

Jack darted out, and Jane looked after him, her eyes brimming. "Twelve years old," she said, "and he doesn't even know his ABC's!"

Brett set his jaw. "We can correct that," he said. "The important thing now is to find out what else he's being taught in place of the basic tools he should have had years ago, and why his teachers have never reported this."

"Maybe he's . . . backward," Jane said fearfully.

"I'm sure he isn't. He's too well-coordinated, and he's got plenty of common sense. We can easily check on that, through one of the remedial reading centers, where they can give him an I.Q. test and fill in the gaps in his alphabet. But in the meantime I'm going to have a good look at that school and our children's teachers, and find out why they haven't caught this thing earlier and advised us to take corrective measures."

After telephoning his office that he would be in later, Brett stopped off at his children's school, arriving while they were still on the playground before their morning classes had begun. First he sought out Jack's teacher, who was surrounded by a group of tough-looking older boys on the playground.

Brett introduced himself to Jack's teacher, a wiry, hard-eyed man whose scarred fingertips showed that his fingernails had once been pulled out.

"Jack's a fine boy, Mr. Cable," the teacher said. "He's a real leader, and he'll go far."

"I'm more interested in his current progress," Brett said, "particularly his reading."

"Oh, don't worry about that," the man said easily, "I'm giving him special instruction in sight-reading. He'll be over the hump before the end of the year."

Brett went next to meet June's teacher, a nervous, white-haired woman who was obviously afraid of several older boys who were laughing hoarsely while they drew obscene pictures on her blackboard.

"Are those boys in your class?" Brett asked.

"Some of them," she said. "The others are from your son's room."

"Can't you do anything about this sort of thing?"

"Mr. Cable, this is nothing compared with what goes on most of the time even when classes are in session."

"You mean there's no classroom discipline—even when the teachers are men?"

"Discipline! It doesn't even exist. Most of the bigger boys carry switch-blade knives, and even the men teachers are afraid to oppose them. Only last year, one man resigned after being slashed when his back was turned."

"How did such a situation ever develop?"

The teacher picked up a worn, paper-backed book, entitled *Teen-age Rebellion.* "Here is their handbook," she said, "and the movie made from it is the pattern they all follow. Most of these children copy the mannerisms of the hoodlums portrayed in the movie, and try to speak like them. It's a cult with them—even to the way they dress and their duck-tail haircuts—a cult of violence and insubordination. It's undermined all our authority, and we've lost control. I wouldn't dare try to stop those boys back there, or they'd make my life miserable for a week."

"Won't the principal back you up?"

"What could he do? He's only one man—and he's old and tired. He's just trying to hang on until he's retired."

"What's the answer? What can we do to help you?"

The woman sighed. "I wish I knew, Mr. Cable. But honestly I don't think there's much anybody can do, now. It's gone too far to stop, and the bigger boys—the real trouble-makers—are in full control. They've got everyone cowed—including the teachers and the principal. I'm giving up. This is my last year. I just can't take it any longer. I've been a teacher all my life, but I'd rather take in washing than put up with what we have to go through. You wouldn't believe me if I told you some of the things

I've seen going on, in the washrooms and even right here in the classroom."

"May I borrow that book? I'd like to see what kind of extra-curricular instruction can produce a situation as bad as this is."

"You can keep it—if you can stomach the thing. I take a dozen copies a month away from the younger girls. The older boys pass the book along after marking the smuttiest pages for the bigger girls to read. Then the older girls—and there's not a virgin among them—teach the younger ones, and taunt them and bully them if they try to stay decent."

"I thought that sort of thing went on only in prisons and reform schools."

"Not any more. There aren't enough corrective institutions in the country to hold a tenth of the lawless teenagers we're raising today." She paused when a bell rang. "Excuse me, Mr. Cable. Now my daily trials begin. I don't know how you're fixed financially, but if you can possibly do it, if I were you I'd get that sweet girl of yours out of this public school before she joins the rest of the pack. By the time she's in high school, it'll be too late to save her."

Back in the Pentagon, Eileen was at her desk when Brett entered the office.

"Good morning, Eileen," he said, perfunctorily. "Would you please get me some black coffee?"

"Certainly, Mr. Cable," she said, noting his preoccupied manner. When she returned with the coffee, Brett was staring out of the window, alone with his unpleasant recollections of the past two hours, frowning slightly.

Eileen put the coffee on his desk, hesitated a moment,

and then said, "Excuse me, Mr. Cable, but you seem upset over something."

Brett looked up, shook his head as if to shake loose from his troubled thoughts, and said, "Yes, frankly, I am."

"Is anything wrong with my work, or have I . . ."

Brett smiled wanly. "Bless you, no. Your work is perfect. Not even a typographical error since you've started. No, this is a personal problem—something entirely new, and basically my fault. I've been pretty blind about something I've been neglecting."

Eileen looked at him questioningly. "If there's anything I can do to help, please let me know."

"Thank you, Eileen. I appreciate that. But don't worry, this doesn't involve your job in any way."

She returned to her desk, and while Brett sipped his coffee and stared out of the window, she sat watching him wistfully for several moments. Suddenly she looked up with a start, to see the Secretary's legal assistant standing in the doorway, watching her with a smile that combined understanding and amusement. She blushed furiously when he wagged an admonitory finger at her and then beckoned silently for her to come through the doorway. She glanced apprehensively at Brett, who was still lost in thought, then walked out of the room.

The legal assistant motioned to the corridor, and when they were outside he said, "How about some coffee, Eileen?"

"I've had some," she said, "and that isn't what you had in mind, anyway. But you're just wasting your time."

"Maybe, but I hate to see you waste yours on Cable. He's not going to give you a tumble. Why keep on kidding yourself? I saw how you looked at him, and he doesn't even know you're around."

"He's upset about something, that's all."

"And you think it's marital frustration, and that he'll pour his troubles into your pretty, sympathetic ear, as an opening gambit for something more exciting."

"Don't be silly!"

"I'm not. I'm serious. How about dinner tonight? And a show afterward?"

"And your apartment after that, of course? No, thanks. I never mix business and pleasure."

"Go on! That adoring light I saw in your eyes when you looked at Cable . . ."

"Stop it. I've got work to do, and please don't bother me again!" She flounced back into the office, and began typing at such a rate that Brett looked up inquiringly at her sudden burst of activity. She avoided his gaze, until he turned back towards his desk. Then she glared at the back of his head, with a look that was unmistakably resentful.

Brett picked up the telephone, dialed his home number, and spoke to Jane: "Hello, darling. I think we'd better move quickly on that problem we discussed. Please call the remedial reading center and make an appointment for Jack—today after he comes home from school. Take a taxicab to the center and leave him there for the tests. They'll take a couple of hours. I'll pick him up on my way home. And see if you can locate this movie for me: it's called 'Teen-age Rebellion.' It's probably playing at one of the cheaper neighborhood theaters in the suburbs, and I want to see it . . . No, we won't take the children to this one. I'll explain when I see you."

CHAPTER TEN

"Don't Miss This Film!"

Brett opened the soiled copy of *Teen-age Rebellion* which his daughter's teacher had given him. He read each of the passages that had been underscored with a pencil, noting that several pages had crude obscene drawings on the margins like those he had seen on the blackboard in the schoolroom.

His telephone rang, and he heard Colonel Howe's voice: "Hello, Brett, how's your schedule this morning?"

"Wide open, Matt. What's up?"

"There's a new Air Force film—a commercial feature, produced with their cooperation—and they've asked for a screen introduction by Secretary Wells, endorsing it as a 'must' for every U.S. citizen. They've set up a preview for their top command at two o'clock this afternoon. Can you come along with me to see it?"

"I'd like to. What's the title of the film, Matt?"

"*Jet Bomber,* from the book of the same name."

"*Jet Bomber!*" Brett repeated, recognizing the title of one of the "Ten Best Books" recommended by editor Lionel Gundy. "This must be my day for movies."

"Why, have you seen it?"

"No, but I've just arranged to see another movie tonight, on a different subject. Who produced the Air Force film, Matt?"

"Sterling Productions, with an all-star cast. They say it's got some great flying scenes. Better come early, if you want a seat. It'll be shown in the main auditorium. They've installed a big panoramic screen just for this occasion, and the place'll be full. I'll come by for you at one forty-five."

"Thanks, Matt. I'll be ready."

When Brett and Matt arrived, the auditorium was nearly filled with high-ranking Air Force officers, while Majors and Captains stood deferentially in the corners of the room. Matt found two seats in a rear row, and everyone stood up as the Chief of Staff was ushered to a reserved seat.

The film opened with some breath-taking full-color scenes of fighter combat high above the clouds during World War II. Next it covered operations with the lumbering B-36 bombers, then it settled down to tell the story of the development of the supersonic jet bomber. The photography was flawless, with magnificent aerial shots that repeatedly drew subdued indications of approval from the audience of professional aviators.

Brett concentrated his attention on the script—particularly the romantic angle. The story was based on the experiences of a Reserve pilot whose career as a rising young executive was twice interrupted by active combat duty, first in World War II and then in the Korean War. His bride, whose part was played by a bosomy blonde, was portrayed as lonely, fearful, and hysterical whenever her husband's plane roared over their jerry-built house towards the stratosphere. The hero's plane repeatedly developed engine trouble, and his plane crew "chickened out," fearful of sabotage. The film's climax was the bomber's emergency landing with two of its engines in flames, after the crew bailed out while the pilot stuck with the controls. The resulting crash injured the pilot, which caused his wife to have a miscarriage and ended his flying career. The closing scene showed the pilot and his wife waving bravely to his squadron mates as they took off on another mission in one of the eight-million-dollar B-52's.

When the film ended, as the lights went on the audience broke into spontaneous applause. Brett glanced at Matt, who was misty-eyed.

"Those are the best damn' flying scenes I ever saw," Matt said as they walked out.

"Yes, they were pretty spectacular," Brett said. "How did you like the rest of the film?"

"Oh, the plot was pretty stupid—typical Hollywood stuff. They haven't had a new plot in twenty years. But those jet bombers—boy, they really caught them just the way they are: a lot of airplane, and a mighty unforgiving one, too."

"A pretty good recruiting film, would you say?" Brett asked casually.

Matt gave him a quick glance, then stopped walking. His animated expression faded, and his face grew serious. "No-o, I don't believe so. I'd call it a great film for *pilots,* but not for *prospective* pilots. I guess I liked it because it didn't pull any punches. It told the truth about flying as it is today. And let's face it: flying supersonic bombers is an exacting, exhausting, dangerous profession. That film didn't exaggerate a thing. It wasn't meant to be a recruiting film, but it did tell an exciting, dramatic story that gripped me from start to finish. I lived through it all again, just seeing it. Why, Brett? What are you getting at?"

"I wanted to get your reactions, and to check them against my own. But you and I and most of the other people who saw that film are a pretty specialized audience, wouldn't you say?"

"I suppose so, but I still say it was one hell of a good movie."

Brett did not press the point. Instead, he walked down to ask Major Joe Tuttle in the Office of Public Relations a question: "Joe, what's the procedure for obtaining the Department's co-operation with the production of a film like *Jet Bomber*? It's all handled right here in OPR, isn't it?"

"That's right, Brett. The movie people submit the idea to the Motion Picture and Television Section, which sounds out the service concerned, and if they like the idea, the studio submits a script—in this case, to the Air Force. Their public relations people go over it for accuracy, then send it back down here to the Security Review Section for final approval."

"They keep copies of the script, I suppose?"

"Right. Every page has to be stamped 'approved' on a carbon copy which is retained in our files."

"Is there an index, or a list of scripts that are in production or pending approval?"

"Sure. Anything you want to look up? Come along, and I'll show you the index." He led the way to a filing cabinet. "Here you are: films completed, scripts approved, ideas submitted, department concerned, and studio requesting co-operation."

Brett leafed through the files until he came to a tab marked "Sterling Productions." In this file he found the script for *Jet Bomber,* approved in forwarding endorsements signed by the Air Force's Director of Public Relations, the Chief of the Strategic Air Command, and the Deputy Secretary of Defense. It also bore enthusiastic endorsements by the Magazine and Book Section and the Director of Public Relations of the Department of Defense. The script had been revised by the author of the book, who had written it in collaboration with an Air Force Major who also served as the film's technical advisor.

Several other scripts submitted by Sterling Productions had also been approved for Department of Defense cooperation. One of these was a Navy film, based on an article written by two Navy Captains on active duty. The article, which was scheduled for early publication in a national weekly magazine, was called "The Navy's Worst Disaster—the Death of the USS *Minneapolis.*"

Brett noted the forwarding endorsements on the article, which had been approved by the Navy's Special Deputy Chief of Public Relations and the Chief of its Magazine and Book Branch. It also carried an approving endorsement signed by the Undersecretary of the Navy.

Among the scripts of movies which had already been filmed by Sterling Productions, Brett found one which carried a screen preview statement by the Secretary of the Air Force, who wrote, "This is the most dramatic combat action ever photographed. *Don't miss this film!*"

Brett studied this script, which was based on a best-selling book called *War in the Orient,* by one of the nation's most successful authors. The story covered some of the bloodiest battles of World War II. The book, Brett recalled, had won the "Best American Fiction" and "Book of the Year" prizes, and the stage version of the hero's romance with a Eurasian girl had made the author rich and famous. The movie script, Brett noticed, also emphasized the miscegenation theme and dwelt on the waste and the futility of war. He had not seen this film, which had been released while he was out of the country.

Brett noted the salient features of each of the scripts, and found several recurring themes. In each story the comic relief was supplied by an enlisted man who outsmarted the officers by evading or ignoring the military regulations which plagued those who were stupid enough to obey them. Dramatic suspense was achieved through situations created by the incompetence, stupidity, or ruthlessness of senior officers who invariably survived, while those who obeyed their orders were either injured, wounded, or killed outright. Enlisted men of another service were referred to in contemptuous terms such as "gobs," "dog-faces," "gyrenes," and "airedales." Each story featured at least one cowardly officer, for whom the enlisted men openly showed their contempt. Enlisted men were portrayed as low-grade morons whose main diversions were lechery and drunken brawls. Service wives were female caricatures who were either unfaithful to their husbands or hopelessly incapable of coping with the stresses of military life. Their children were ill, neglected, or heart-sick waifs whose lives were warped by parental misunderstandings between wives who wanted "a real home" and husbands who stubbornly ignored everything but blind adherence to military traditions.

In order to check his reactions, Brett purchased copies of several of the books which had been filmed. After underlining similar passages in the books, he compared these with the screen dialogue from the films, and found virtually all of the screen dialogue quoted directly from the books.

Returning to his office, Brett dictated a short memorandum to Eileen: "The passages marked in the attached book appear virtually without change in the script for the motion picture of the same name which was produced by Sterling Productions with the approval and co-operation of the Department of Defense. These scripts are on file in the Motion Picture and Television Section of OPR/DD."

"Who shall I send this to?" Eileen asked.

"Don't send it," Brett said. "Just mark it 'Memorandum for Record' and file a copy of it with each of these books, and put them in the bottom drawer of the filing cabinet on top of the magazines I've left there."

Brett picked up a Washington newspaper and turned to the amusement pages. As he anticipated, *War in the Orient* was still being shown, in one of the suburban neighborhood movie houses. Picking up the telephone, he called Jane.

"Hello, darling," he said. "Have you located the movie I asked you about?"

"Yes, Brett. It's playing at the Abraham Lincoln theater in southeast Washington. I asked one of our neighbors where that is, and she says it's in a very tough neighborhood, where it's unsafe to walk alone after dark. Are you sure we ought to go there?"

"We won't have to. I've seen the book, which is bad enough, and I understand the movie is even more depressing. I've found another one I'd like to see instead. It's an aviation film, and we can take the children to this one. It's called *War in the Orient*."

"Oh, good! The stage version had some lovely music, and I've always wanted to see the film."

"Fine. Let's eat early and we'll go to the first show. I'll pick Jack up on my way home."

Leaving the office earlier than usual, Brett drove over to the remedial reading center in Washington, where he found Jack waiting in the director's office.

"Quite a boy you've got there, Mr. Cable," the director said. "He's told me all about your fine war record."

"I haven't been doing so well with my peace-time responsibilities, I'm afraid," Brett said.

"I wouldn't say that," the director said. "At least you have a son who likes you, respects you, and has stood up for you with his fists against boys armed with knives."

Brett's eyes widened. "I didn't realize that. Jack, you never told me."

Jack grinned happily and rolled up his left sleeve to show his father a partly-healed cut below the elbow. "Didn't hurt a bit," he said. "The punk didn't even know how to use a knife, and I cooled him before he could rake me. So I didn't think I'd bother you."

"When was this, son, and how did it happen?"

"About a week ago. This hood called you a lousy stinking Marine, I clipped him, and he pulled his switch-blade. Then I really let him have it."

"Does your teacher know this?"

"Sure. He saw it. It was right in his room, while we were at the blackboard. The teacher put a bandage on it, and told me not to tell anybody, or they'd think I was chicken."

The director handed Jack a quarter and said, "There's a drug store at the corner, Jack. Get yourself some ice cream, and thanks for being so patient during the tests we gave you. I want to go over them with your father."

"Gee, thanks a lot!" Jack said, and looked inquiringly at his father.

"Go ahead, son," Brett said. "You can wait for me in the drug store."

After Jack left, the director glanced at the papers in front of him and asked, "Mr. Cable, do you know anything about 'progressive' education?"

"Not very much," Brett said, "but I'm beginning to learn. I never heard the term until yesterday, when I found out that my son couldn't read. That's why we came to you for help."

"You're fortunate. Some parents never realize what's going on until their children are in high school. By that time it's usually too late for us to be of much help. Your son's case is fairly simple. He's a bright lad, with a high I.Q. There's nothing wrong with his mind, I can assure you."

Brett exhaled with relief. "Thank God for that. You never know, when you're suddenly confronted with a situation like this."

"It's a normal reaction. Most parents think their children may be subnormal, when this sort of case crops up —and we get them by the hundreds. Mr. Cable, have you any idea how your son got so far behind without your realizing it until now?"

"Yes, I have. The grading system is so vague these days that neither the children nor their parents know what progress the child is making. Jack should have received failing grades long ago, which would have alerted us. Instead, he was passed along with no indication that his work was unsatisfactory and that he didn't even know his ABC's."

"That's only part of it. He can't add, subtract, multiply or divide. Our tests show that he's never learned his multiplication tables even up through the tens—which is as far as they're taught in most public schools today. In my day we were taught through the fifteens, and later it was reduced to the twelves."

"Why? Who lowered the standards?"

"It's a long story. But here's one reason: if you can multiply only through the tens, you can easily revert to counting on your fingers. And if you're permitted and encouraged to use printing and disjointed letters instead of the cursive or flowing handwriting you and I were taught with copybooks, it'll slow down your thinking and your ability to express yourself articulately."

Brett paused and chose his words carefully. "Do you mean that our children are being deliberately undereducated—intentionally?"

The director looked at him searchingly for a moment, then said, "Yes, Mr. Cable. That's exactly what I mean. I believe I can trust you not to quote me?"

"You can."

"You've already put your finger on the basic evil, which is the promotion of the unqualified and the unfit, without any indication to their parents that their children aren't even being taught the 'three R's.' But that's only part of the pattern. In traditional education both the child and his parents have a constant check on his progress through daily or weekly grades. Competition is encouraged, and outstanding performance receives special recognition. Failure to meet a reasonable standard—it used to be 75 per cent, but now its as low as 65 or even 60—means that the child fails the course and is not promoted unless he makes up the work. In 'progressive' education, the opposite is true: competition is discouraged, mediocrity is acceptable, and everyone passes the course and is promoted. Personal excellence is discouraged, and the ambitious student is soon dragged down to the average level of the group."

"How about classroom discipline?"

The director smiled. "Now you're getting to the real root of the problem. In traditional education the teacher's authority is absolute. Attendance and full attention are mandatory at all times. Not even minor infractions of classroom discipline are tolerated. Insubordination or impudence means expulsion, and the teacher is backed to the hilt. Children learn to rely on their elders for guidance and authority. In 'progressive' classrooms discipline is almost non-existent. Children are allowed to talk to each other, to interrupt when others are reciting, and even to interrupt the teacher. Those who try to maintain order are ridiculed and discouraged. Respect for authority decreases to the point of delinquency."

"What happens when it finally becomes obvious that a boy like Jack just can't do the work he's assigned—that he's failing?"

"In a 'progressive' school the child is protected against a sense of failure as long as possible. This is supposed to aid his 'social and emotional growth.' If he reaches high school, he's carried along with the others until the second or third year. By that time his case is hopeless, his parents are advised that he's 'not college material' and he is assigned to the 'industrial' group—along with the other failures and misfits.

"Up to that time he's had easy going. Then he's brought face to face with reality for the first time, and it's a rude shock. He's had his heart set on all the wonderful and desirable possessions he's seen in the movies and on television—motor-boats, convertibles, airplanes, pretty girls. Suddenly he realizes he'll never get any of them on a garage mechanic's pay, and that he can't even afford to marry the bobby-soxer he's been going steady with, ever since she was twelve years old. If his parents are college-educated, it's a severe traumatic experience for them as well as for him."

"How do most children react to such an experience?"

"It depends on their age. The older the child, the worse it is. When an over-protected adolescent is unprepared to cope with failure in adult life, he may react to failure either by cracking up, or by turning to anyone who offers him security—no matter what he loses in self-respect or personal freedom."

"In other words, he might welcome a planned economy —or even a police state?"

"Exactly. 'Progressive' education is education for socialism."

"And socialism is only a euphemism for communism."

"That's right, Mr. Cable. Now you know what your son was headed for."

"Can we stop it?"

"Yes. As I said, he's one of the lucky ones; you caught it in time. His case is comparatively simple: a few reversals, and the usual substitutions for the gaps in his syllabication. He's had no phonetics, and we'll correct that in no time. At first we'd like to see him at least four times a week, for an hour a day. Later on, we can cut that down to twice a week, plus homework. He should be able to read at the third grade level within ten weeks, and it shouldn't take more than a year to bring him up to sixth grade level, both in reading and arithmetic. His writing will take longer; he'll really have to start all over, and work hard at it."

"What will this cost?"

"Here's a schedule of our fees. We try to keep them as low as possible, and to arrange payments on the same basis that most doctors do. And it will be a pleasure to work with a boy like yours. You must have a very happy home life."

"Thank you. We do. And I can't tell you how much I appreciate what you're doing for me and my son."

That evening, without prior comment, Brett took Jane and their children to see *War in the Orient.* The flying scenes were superbly filmed, and the musical score was filled with familiar numbers from the stage version. As the plot built up in dramatic intensity, Brett covertly observed the instinctive revulsion of his family to scenes of brutality, violence and death. As they left the theater, Brett asked casually, "How did you like the picture?"

Jack spoke first: "I don't think I'd like to be a pilot, if that's the way it was."

"How do you mean?" Brett asked.

"Well, after all that fellow did, shooting down planes, knocking out tanks, blowing up bridges—then he gets forced down trying to help that no-good guy, and ends up being shot down by a bunch of Gooks in a dirty old sewage ditch."

June said, "I don't think I'd want to be married to an Air Force man, Daddy."

"Why not?"

"Well . . . I just wouldn't want to *be* a widow."

Brett turned to his wife. "How about you, darling. Did you like the picture?"

Jane looked at him strangely. "Did you know it would be like that? I thought people went to the movies to be *entertained.* Please, Brett, let's hurry home. I think I'm going to be sick."

CHAPTER ELEVEN

A Question of Identity

After several days had passed without any word from Undersecretary Hale's office about the CCC pageant, Brett called on Fred Gruber and asked about the status of the Pastor-Chaplain program.

"It's making great progress," Gruber said. "The program should be of real assistance to our recruitment activities, with all the publicity it's getting."

"What about the pageant they planned to use?" Brett asked, standing in front of Gruber's desk.

"It will be an integral part of the program," Gruber said blandly.

"You mean it's been *approved?*" Brett asked, incredulously.

"Yes, Mr. Cable, I do. As I told you before, it has received careful consideration. I reviewed it myself, and found nothing objectionable from an aesthetic viewpoint. I've approved the entire program, and I've accepted the CCC's invitation for Undersecretary Hale to speak on the role of the service wife—which is a vital part of their indoctrination program. I understand that you're preparing a report on the project for Secretary Wells, who is returning tomorrow with Mr. Hale. Is your report completed?"

"Not until Secretary Wells has signed it."

"Naturally. I'd appreciate having a copy as soon as it's

signed, to enclose with my report to Mr. Hale. Thank you for coming in, Mr. Cable," Gruber said, nodding curtly, and picking up his telephone. "Now, if you'll excuse me, I'm already late for another appointment."

Outwardly calm, Brett stood for a moment and looked at Gruber, who swung his chair sideways to face his telephone, avoiding Brett's penetrating gaze.

"Certainly, Mr. Gruber," he said. "Sorry to have bothered you."

Brett went immediately to the Pentagon Library, where he searched through the files for other works by the pageant's author, Michael Irwin. Finding none, he turned to the reference books. Finally, in a volume called *Who's Who in American Literature,* he found Irwin's name listed with the notation: "Pseudonym of author Irving Solomen." Under the latter name, Brett found a long biography with a list of several anti-capitalist books and plays, some of them written in Russian. Solomen was also an avid joiner, with membership in numerous organizations including two which had been cited by the U.S. Attorney General as Communist "fronts."

Brett copied the biography and took it to Mead Jayson in MID. As he read the biography, Jayson's attitude of patient indulgence changed to one of alert concern.

"Where did you get this information, Mr. Cable?"

"In the Pentagon Library, from *Who's Who in American Literature*. Don't you have a copy in MID?"

"Unfortunately, no. But this changes the whole picture—especially these two organizations on the Attorney General's list."

Jayson then introduced Brett to Merle Dawson, the GBS liaison officer assigned to the Pentagon, and explained the situation.

Dawson scanned the biography and telephoned GBS

headquarters for a name-check on Irving Solomen. After hearing the report, Dawson said gravely, "This case is dynamite. Solomen's red hot. The report on him is classified EYES ONLY. They're sending it over by special courier. I'll wait for it here, and in the meantime I'd like to hear more about this CCC outfit."

While Dawson took notes, Brett described the CCC's Pastor-Chaplain program and the DSI evaluation of the pageant which had been written for it.

When the GBS report arrived, Dawson glanced through it and handed it to Brett without comment. The file showed that Irving Solomen not only had a long record of active co-operation with Communist-front organizations, but that he was currently under GBS surveillance for espionage for the USSR, having recently met with known Communists actively engaged in infiltrating the top echelons of the U.S. government.

Brett read the file and handed it to Mead Jayson, who paused half-way through it and said, "Mr. Cable, I think Secretary Wells ought to see this file as soon as he returns. In the meantime you'd better take steps to protect Undersecretary Hale from getting further involved in this mess. I'll hang onto the file and show it to Secretary Wells. And thank you for the lead on the real identity of the fellow who wrote that pageant. Without your tip-off, we'd have missed him completely."

Brett returned to the office of Fred Gruber, who looked up with an annoyed expression.

"Yes, Mr. Cable, what is it now?"

"It's about the Philadelphia pageant, Mr. Gruber."

"Well, what about it, Mr. Cable?"

"The author is the subject of a GBS report in the EYES ONLY category. MID suggested that Undersecretary

Hale's office be notified, and I understand that you're acting for him in his absence."

Gruber flushed slowly to the roots of his hair. "Thank you for telling me, Mr. Cable," he said, with a visible effort to maintain his composure. "May I see this report?"

"I don't have it. It was shown to me by Merle Dawson of the GBS."

"I see," Gruber said calmly. "In that case, you'd better take whatever corrective measures you think appropriate under the circumstances, since you obviously are better informed than I am."

"Where would you suggest that I start?"

"That's up to you. But I should point out that so many high government officials have endorsed this program that it would be unwise to cancel it entirely. Too much unfavorable publicity would result. Too many of our people are committed to participation, for us to back out now."

"I'm afraid so," Brett agreed. "But don't we also have an obligation to the public? The least we can do is to protect the civic officials and the religious groups who are being taken in by this thing, by stopping the pageant. After all, military personnel are taking part in it, and they're under the jurisdiction of this Department and of your office."

"That's true. But we can't inform the Philadelphia officials about the pageant. That would violate security regulations."

"Not necessarily. With the authority of your office it can be done very easily."

"Very well, Mr. Cable. You may use that authority—provided that you accept full responsibility for your actions and the results. What do you propose to do?"

"May I use your telephone?"

"Certainly. But you're responsible for any security violations."

Brett telephoned the Chairman of the Philadelphia Civic Affairs Committee, explained that he was calling from Undersecretary Hale's office, and requested that the pageant be deleted from the program.

"We can't do that," the Chairman protested. "A huge cast—several hundred people from schools, churches, and civic organizations—has been rehearsing it, and more than half our budget has already been spent on it. Furthermore, the pageant is the backbone of the entire program, which is based on television distribution of films of the pageant. If you had any objections to it, why weren't we told weeks ago? Everybody up here thinks it's just great. What's wrong with it?"

"I'm sorry," Brett said, "but all I'm authorized to tell you is that the script is unacceptable to the Department of Defense." He glanced at Gruber, who nodded in agreement.

"That's not enough!" the Chairman said angrily. "Unless you can give us a better reason than that, we're going ahead with it."

"In that case," Brett said, "no U.S. military personnel on active duty will be permitted to attend the conference or take part in the program." Again he glanced inquiringly at Gruber, who hesitated momentarily and then slowly nodded in reluctant approval. "And that includes all military chaplains," Brett added.

"All right," the Chairman said grudgingly. "We'll delete the pageant, if the Defense Department will provide a suitable substitute which can be used later on television."

Brett relayed this proposal to Gruber, who approved

it, adding that there were plenty of military films which could be substituted for the pageant, and that appropriate material could also be worked into Undersecretary Hale's speech, which could also be televised. The Chairman accepted this compromise, but reminded Brett that time was short, with only two weeks before the opening of the Pastor-Chaplain Conference.

After leaving Gruber's office, Brett dictated a memorandum for record covering the day's activities. Eileen's eyebrows raised as she took the notes in shorthand.

"Please stamp that *Confidential,*" Brett said, "and file it with the classified material in my safe."

After Eileen left, Brett stayed on until he had cleared up the routine material in his incoming basket, then locked his safe and checked the combination lock. As he left the building, dusk had set in and the corridors were empty except for the guard at the reception desk.

Following his customary route, Brett walked diagonally across the Pentagon parking area, which was almost empty, towards his assigned parking space. Suddenly a large car without lights sped directly towards him, its engine roaring. Diving out of the way at the last possible moment, Brett escaped being run down only by rolling on the pavement. He had only a fleeting glimpse of the big car, which he recognized as a government limousine. With its tires screeching the darkened car careened to the end of the parking area before its lights were turned on, too far away for Brett to be able to make out its license number.

Getting to his feet, Brett dusted himself off and walked rapidly to his own car, somewhat shaken by the realization that someone deliberately had tried to run him down.

CHAPTER TWELVE

The Pattern Develops

Early the next morning Undersecretary Hale and Secretary Wells returned from their overseas inspection trip. Colonel Howe met their plane at the Washington International Airport, only a five-minute drive from the Pentagon, and accompanied Secretary Wells to his office, where Wells immediately sent for Brett.

"I understand Mead Jayson of MID is waiting to see me at once on an urgent matter," Wells told Brett. "What's it all about?"

Brett explained briefly about the Pastor-Chaplain Program of the Civilian Council of Churches, and the pageant which had been submitted as the basis for a nationwide indoctrination program involving military morale. He then showed Wells the evaluation of the pageant by the Division of Special Investigations.

Wells' eyebrows raised as he read the DSI report. "Ask Jayson to come in at once," he told Colonel Howe.

Jayson entered and said, "Good morning, Mr. Secretary. Sorry to bother you the moment you return, but the Director thought you ought to see this GBS file as soon as possible." He handed Wells the EYES ONLY file on Irving Solomen.

Wells read the file rapidly but intently, then turned to

Jayson and said, "This is quite a dossier. This fellow seems to be a very high-level operator."

"That's right, sir," Jayson said. "It could have been extremely embarrassing to everyone concerned—particularly to your office—if this program had been subverted for anti-morale purposes. Solomen's real identity was the key to the whole scheme, and Mr. Cable deserves full credit for the lead which exposed Solomen when we couldn't trace the pseudonym he was using."

Wells looked at Brett with an expression of surprise. "Well, Brett, I didn't know you were an intelligence expert, along with your other accomplishments. Have you had any training in that field?"

"No, Mr. Secretary," Brett said. "I was just checking my sources, like any other newspaper man would do, and I happened to run across the right reference book. My recommendations to you on this project wouldn't have made much sense with a gap like that in my report."

Jayson smiled. "I think we'd better hire a few newspaper men in MID, Mr. Secretary. Maybe they could show us a few short-cuts."

"Not a bad idea," Wells said. "Nice work, Brett. I'm glad you stopped this thing before it got out of control. And thanks for making your story brief, with all the paper-work that's piled up in my absence. Just look at that incoming stack! I've been away much too long. Thanks for coming in, Mr. Jayson. And here's your file. We don't want anything like that lying around this office. By the way, what action will your office take in Solomen's case?"

"We can't touch him," Jayson said. "As a civilian, he comes under GBS jurisdiction. But he's a smart operator, and has always managed to avoid anything illegal enough to give the government a real case against him. But this time he's come pretty close to the danger line—which he'll realize as soon as he learns that his pageant has been dropped from the program. A blunder like that will end his effectiveness, as far as our area is concerned. I don't think we'll hear anything more about him for a long, long time—at least for a couple of years, and never again in the military field."

"Well, thank Heaven the case is closed, as far as we're concerned," Wells said. "Now we can get back to the really important things and do the work that's cut out for us."

After Jayson left, Wells said to Brett, "Now, here's something Stacy Hale and I worked up during our return trip. We both feel there's a real need for a public declaration of what the Department of Defense stands for—its roles and missions, its capabilities and responsibilities—a re-statement of everything basic about the country's Armed Forces, not only for our own people, but to serve notice also to the enemy that we won't tolerate any foolishness." He took a folded sheet of paper out of his inside pocket. "We've worked hard on this thing, and I believe we've just about got it, except for a bit of polishing. Here, let me read it to you."

Holding the paper at arm's length, Wells read in a firm, resonant voice: "The U.S. Armed Forces are the guardians of our country. The Department of Defense is responsible for maintaining the nation's fighting forces in readiness at home and overseas, capable of strong action to preserve the peace or of instant offensive action to win in war.

"We serve with honor. Tradition, valor and victory are

our heritage from the past. To these may be added dedication, discipline and vigilance as the watchwords of the present and the future.

"At home or on distant stations we serve with pride, confident in the respect of our country, our comrades in arms, and our families. Our responsibilities sober us; our adversities strengthen us. Service to God and country is our special privilege.

"Our Armed Forces will always employ new weapons, new techniques, and greater power to protect and defend the United States on the land, on the sea and under the sea, and in the air. The roots of our nation lie in a strong belief in the future, in continued dedication to our tasks and in reflection on our heritage from the past. Never have our opportunities and our responsibilities been greater."

Wells handed the paper to Brett and said, "That's about it. I want every man in uniform to have a copy of it. We can send this message to all of our unit commanders on Armed Forces Day and have them read it to their men. Our people have got to know what they're fighting for, and why. Let's send this to all of the key service publications—particularly the public relations newsletters—with a directive to add it to their mastheads as a permanent feature of every issue. Please prepare a directive to that effect for my signature, to go along with the message."

The telephone rang, and Wells picked up the receiver. "Oh, hello, Stacy . . . sorry I'm late. I'll be right down." He nodded to Brett, indicating that he had no further instructions, and Brett left the office as Wells spoke to Colonel Howe over the intercom: "Hello, Matt? Please call the barber shop and get me an appointment for a haircut and tell my wife I won't be home for dinner and may be here quite late—probably every night for the rest of the week, until I catch up with this paper-work."

As Brett passed Colonel Howe's office, Matt called through the open door: "Hey, Brett, I just had a call from the editor of *Our Armed Forces*. He wants to know when he can expect that article by Secretary Wells. And here's a note from the Chief of the Air Force about that endorsement for *Jet Bomber*. I'll have to give Mr. Wells a status report on both projects today. How are they coming along?"

"I'm still working on both items, Matt, but there are a couple of points I'd like to check with Secretary Wells before I can submit either project as completed staff work. Could I see him for about ten minutes this afternoon?"

Matt looked at his appointment pad. "I'm afraid not, Brett. He's booked up solid. How about the first thing in the morning—before he gets caught in the daily rat-race—about eight-fifteen?"

"All right, Matt. I'll have everything ready for him before I leave tonight."

Returning to his office, Brett checked back through Irving Solomen's biography, listing the titles of each of the books and plays Solomen had written. Comparing this list with the list of films produced with the cooperation of the Department of Defense, Brett found that two of Solomen's plays had been filmed by Sterling Productions. The first, called *Death of a Counterspy,* listed a U.S. Army Colonel as its technical advisor. Consulting his Pentagon directory, Brett found that the Colonel was currently on duty with MID in the Pentagon.

The second film, called *Underground Operator,* listed as its technical advisor a U.S. Navy Commander who was now in charge of the Magazine and Book Section of the Office of Public Relations of the Department of Defense —OPR/DD.

Brett swung his chair around toward Eileen, who looked up inquiringly from her typewriter.

"Eileen," he said, "I'm racing a couple of deadlines. Would you please get me a copy of the latest issue of *Our Armed Forces* Magazine? I'd send a messenger from the mail room, but I need it right away. It's issued every other week."

"Certainly, Mr. Cable. I can get one at the magazine stand on the concourse."

"Try OPR first. They're closer, and they usually get an advance copy before it's on the news-stands."

As soon as Eileen returned with the magazine, Brett turned to its list of recommended movies. In addition to its regular feature "The Ten Best Films" there was a special review on the same page headed "*Jet Bomber*—the USAF's Greatest Film." This review was signed by the magazine's editor, Lionel Gundy, who predicted that its star, a former USAF Ace, would win an Academy Award for his sympathetic portrayal of a Reserve pilot whose wife breaks under the strain of his nerve-racking flights. Gundy's review also contained an "exclusive announcement" which stated that the film credits would contain an enthusiastic endorsement by the Honorable J. Hardy Wells, Assistant Secretary of Defense for Military Morale—information which obviously had been "leaked" by a Pentagon source.

To check the source of this leak, Brett went first to the Motion Picture and Television Section of the Air Force's Office of Public Relations. There he asked the officer-in-charge for copies of the latest newsletters and bulletins to

Air Force field activities. None of these publications contained any mention of *Jet Bomber,* but the Public Relations Newsletter contained a feature which caught Brett's eye at once: "Recommended Books, Movies, and Magazine Articles."

Brett compared the recommended items with those recommended by *Our Armed Forces* and found many duplications. In addition, he found that most of the recommended articles were written by Air Force personnel and had appeared in magazines published by Dawn Publications. As he studied the papers and magazines spread out on his desk, he perceived their significance like the pattern of a photograph which emerges in the developing fluid—unrecognizable at first, then clear and unmistakable.

As the full realization of his discovery swept over him, Brett gave an involuntary gasp.

Eileen turned to see him staring at the Air Force Newsletter clutched in his hands. "What is it, Mr. Cable?" she asked, worriedly. "You're not ill, are you?"

Brett turned to her with a tense expression. "No, but I need your help, and I haven't got much time. Eileen, I want you to get me copies of the Public Relations Newsletters issued by the Army, the Navy, and the Marine Corps—the last four issues of each one. I need them today—urgently. Call each activity and request delivery, if necessary, by officer messenger. When they're delivered, please go through each copy with a blue pencil and underline all references to books, magazine articles, movies, plays, television programs—anything in the information, education, or amusement fields. I'm going down to OPR. If you run into any road-blocks, call me at Major Joe Tuttle's desk." He paused, noting her expression of increasing concern, then smiled and said, "Don't worry, Eileen. This doesn't affect you or your job in any way. It may not make even any sense to you—but please believe me, it's important, and I'm depending on you. Any questions—about what I want or where to get it?"

She shook her head dubiously and said, "No-o."

"Good!" he said. "You know where to reach me."

Brett hurried down to the Office of Public Relations of the Department of Defense. Major Joe Tuttle was not at his desk, and his secretary said that he was attending a press briefing.

Brett walked through OPR to the Magazine and Book Section, where a Wave secretary was seated at a desk by the door.

"Can I help you?" she asked.

"Yes, please," Brett said. "I'd like to see the officer-in-charge."

"I'm sorry, but the Commander is proof-reading just now, and left orders not to be disturbed." She nodded towards a closed door at the end of the room. "If it's something urgent, I can interrupt him."

"That won't be necessary," Brett said. "Maybe you can help me. I'm from Undersecretary Wells' office, and I'm working on an announcement he wants published in the newsletters and bulletins which go to all field activities. Each of the services publishes its own, and I understand they're printed somewhere in the Pentagon."

"That's right, sir, in the Pentagon Publications Section, two floors below us in the sub-basement. They also publish our bulletins, which go to each of the service Book and Magazine Sections. Here's a copy of this week's issue."

She handed Brett a two-page newsletter. He glanced at

it casually and said, "I suppose your office co-ordinates most of the activities in this field."

"That's right. The editors and publishers contact us and outline their needs. We have a huge backlog of requests for stories and articles on military subjects, and we provide most of the leads for servicemen whose work is published. We also send our weekly bulletins to all the other U.S. Government Departments and to a long list of military publications and company house-organs published by defense contractors, which gives us nationwide coverage."

"All this must keep you pretty busy."

"Oh, my, yes. The Commander really ought to have a couple of assistants, but somehow he manages to do all the work himself. I never saw anyone so dedicated to his work. He sleeps only about four hours each night. But apparently he thrives on it."

"I'd like to meet him some time," Brett said. "By the way, have you any extra copies of your bulletin—the last four or five issues?"

"Certainly. Here you are. And please call on us any time we can be of service. The Commander's in New York several days each week, contacting the editors and publishers, so it might be best to call first for an appointment."

"Is the Commander by any chance an author, too?"

"Oh, yes. He's written several best-sellers. Haven't you read his latest book, *The Un-Nautical Crew*? It's been sold to the movies."

"I've seen book reviews of it," Brett said. "Who's producing the film?"

"Sterling Productions. You really ought to read it. There's a laugh on every page."

"Thanks for the tip," Brett said, "and thanks for the bulletins. Now, about the Pentagon Publications Section, is that a branch of OPR?"

"No, they're a sort of an orphan outfit. They were set up just last year, after a publications survey by the Undersecretary's office recommended consolidation of all Pentagon publications under a single staff."

"Who do they report to?"

"They report directly to Mr. Gruber, the Undersecretary's Special Assistant. He was the one who made the change, and it certainly saves us a lot of headaches. All we have to do now is to turn our copy over to them, and they print and distribute it."

"Sounds like a very efficient operation," Brett said. "Thanks for educating me."

"Not at all," she said, with an engaging smile. "Come back any time."

Brett returned to his office, where Eileen was checking the newsletters which had been delivered.

"Did you run into any snags?" he asked.

"No," she said, "they were all delivered promptly. And it's really very simple, because they're so much alike. I've checked all but three, and I'll have those finished in a few minutes."

Brett took the stack of newsletters and turned to the pages Eileen had marked with a blue pencil. Except for minor variations in style and layout, the Army, Navy and Marine Corps Public Relations Newsletters differed very little from those issued by the Air Force and the Department of Defense. Each had a section devoted to books, movies, television programs, and magazine articles of interest to its own personnel. When he compared each recommended item with those endorsed by *Our Armed*

Forces, Brett found the same pattern of duplications he had observed in the Air Force Public Relations Newsletter.

As he studied the interlocking relationships of the publications on his desk, Brett listed each recurring item on a sheet of note-paper. After consulting his notes he turned to Eileen and asked, "Have you ever typed directly from dictation?"

"Yes, but I'm not very fast at it."

"I'll go slowly. This is only a rough draft of a report which I'll revise later. Just the original—no carbons. First I'll give you a list of motion picture titles, which you can list in a column. After each title, I'll give you the name of the military department whose facilities were used or whose personnel assisted in its production."

Brett dictated from his notes, while Eileen typed as follows:

I. *Motion Pictures produced by Sterling Productions with the cooperation of the Armed Services*

1. *Death of a Counterspy* — U.S. Army. Author: Irving Solomen*
2. *Battle for Burma* — U.S. Army.
3. *No One Escaped* — U.S. Army.
4. *The West Point Saga* — U.S. Army.
5. *Hillbilly Sergeant* — U.S. Army.
6. *Underground Operator* — U.S. Navy. Author: Irving Solomen*
7. *Suicide Run to Murmansk* — U.S. Navy.
8. *War in the Orient* — U.S. Navy and U.S. Marine Corps.

* See Philadelphia Pageant, below.

9. *Mutiny at Sea*	U.S. Navy.
10. *The Kamikaze Attacks*	U.S. Navy.
11. *Annapolis Log*	U.S. Navy.
12. *The Tokyo Raid*	U.S. Air Force and U.S. Navy.
13. *Prisoner of War*	U.S. Air Force.
14. *Rear Gunner*	U.S. Air Force.
15. *Jet Bomber*	U.S. Air Force.
16. *The Marines Have Landed*	U.S. Marine Corps.

Scheduled for Production

1. *The Un-Nautical Crew*	U.S. Navy.
2. *Too Late for Corporals*	U.S. Army.
3. *Guided Missile*	U.S. Air Force.

(All of these movies have been endorsed and approved by the service concerned and by the Office of Public Relations of the Department of Defense)

Non-Military Films Produced by Sterling Productions

1. *Teen-age Rebellion*
2. *Switch-Blade Knife*
3. *Crossing the Color Line*
4. *Call-House Queen*

Note: All of the foregoing productions have been endorsed for military personnel by *Our Armed Forces* Magazine.

II. *Stories and articles by military personnel*

1. Published by Dawn Publications (16 magazines)*
2. Endorsed by *Our Armed Forces* and the Public Relations Newsletters of the Armed Services and the Department of Defense.
3. Distributed by Pentagon magazine stand and drug store, by stores operated by the Armed Services, by drug stores, stationery stores, chain groceries, and by the libraries of public schools.

* Note: See *Battle Horror Publications* file in MID, labeled subversive by DSI. Corrective action prevented by the Director of Public Relations of the Department of Defense.

III. *Philadelphia Pageant* (labeled subversive by DSI)

1. Author: Irving Solomen*
2. Endorsed by the Civilian Council of Churches, military chaplains of the Army, Navy, and Air Force, and the Special Assistant to the Undersecretary of Defense for Industrial Mobilization.
3. Basis for the nationwide Pastor-Chaplain Program of indoctrination for teen-age draftees, which has White House approval.
4. Scheduled to attend: Undersecretary of Defense Hale and the Vice President of the United States.

* Subject of GBS EYES ONLY report in espionage category. See also movies 1 and 6, above.

IV. *Requests for endorsements by Assistant Secretary Wells*

1. Article for *Our Armed Forces* on "The Problems of Military Morale."

2. Endorsement of motion picture *Jet Bomber* as "a *must* for every U.S. citizen."

   (Advance information on this request leaked to *Our Armed Forces* Magazine by a Pentagon source.)

V. *Endorsement of OUR ARMED FORCES Magazine by the Director of Public Relations of the Department of Defense*

1. In a memorandum to the Assistant Secretary of Defense for Military Morale (ADS/MM) the Director of Public Relations of the Department of Defense (DPR/DD) endorsed a request by the editor of *Our Armed Forces* Magazine for an article to be signed by ASD/MM, as follows:

   From: Director of Public Relations
   To: Assistant Secretary of Defense for Military Morale
   Subject: Attached request from OUR ARMED FORCES Magazine for an article entitled "The Problems of Military Morale."

   (1) OUR ARMED FORCES Magazine is an excellent medium of communications for purposes of internal dissemination of information to servicemen and their families even though it is an "outside" publication.
   (2) OUR ARMED FORCES co-operates with and supports the general objectives of the Office of Public Relations.
   (3) The Office of Public Relations co-operates fully with OUR ARMED FORCES.
   (4) It is recommended that you provide OUR

> ARMED FORCES with the article requested in the attached letter. It is further recommended that, since this request is from an "outside" publication and is addressed to this office, you submit the requested article to this office for review and clearance for the record.

At this point in Brett's dictation the telephone rang, and Eileen picked up the receiver. She listened for a moment and then turned to Brett with a white face.

"It's Mr. Gruber's secretary," she said. "She wants to know if it would be convenient for you to see him in his office for a few minutes."

Brett's nostrils flared slightly, then he said quietly, "Yes. Tell her I'll be right down."

CHAPTER THIRTEEN

Undersecretary Hale's Speech

When Brett entered Fred Gruber's office, Gruber was standing by a filing cabinet, which he closed as Brett came through the doorway.

"Oh, hello, Mr. Cable," Gruber said affably. "Thanks for coming in. Won't you please sit down?" He indicated a chair at the side of his desk, and when both men were seated, he continued: "Here's a copy of a speech I've prepared for Mr. Hale to deliver at the Pastor-Chaplain Conference. I'd be grateful if you'd look it over and return it with any comments, criticisms or suggestions you may have. I know this is a rather unusual request, but after our experience with that pageant—well, I just want to make sure that nothing we say or do will offend anyone in any way."

He handed Brett a folder labeled "*The Service Wife,* an address by the Honorable Stacy Hale, Undersecretary of Defense for Industrial Mobilization, for delivery before the Pastor-Chaplain Conference of the Civilian Council of Churches."

"Actually," Gruber said, "it would have been much more appropriate for someone from Military Morale or Personnel to deliver a speech like this, but the White House asked for the most senior Defense official available, and Mr. Hale was tapped for the assignment. In any case, we thought you ought to see it."

"We?" Brett repeated.

"The Undersecretary and I. Secretary Wells speaks very highly of your ability as a speech-writer, and we'd be grateful for an expert's opinion, in an event as important as this."

"I'm highly flattered," Brett said, "but I've got two other deadlines to meet by tomorrow morning. When do you want this back?"

"Today, if possible. It's not a long speech; you can read it in fifteen minutes. And please let me emphasize that this is only an informal request. Normally, we'd have checked first to see if it was all right with Mr. Wells. We can still do so, if you insist."

"You might not be able to reach him for an hour, and I can have this back to you before that."

"Good! I'll really appreciate it. If you want to save time, you can dictate your comments to my secretary in the next room. Please make yourself at home, and call me if I can be of any assistance."

"Thanks. That will be much quicker."

Brett took the folder into the adjacent room and studied the speech carefully, taking notes as he did so. When he finished, he turned to Gruber's secretary and dictated a brief memorandum for Gruber: "This speech does not appear to be well suited to its prospective audience, which will be predominantly civilian rather than military. There is too much emphasis on inadequate housing, lack of medical care for dependents, and financial hardships—factors which have drastically lowered our reenlistment rates and which we are now trying to play down until they can be corrected by legislative action which already has been introduced. The overall effect of this speech is to play up the drawbacks of peace-time married life in the Armed Services without offering any inducement beyond patriotic duty—which appears inappropriate for an audience made up of the parents of teenage draftees who are unmarried when they enter military service. Instead of emphasizing these negative aspects, a more constructive approach would be to point out some of the advantages of military service which are listed in the pamphlet issued by the Office of Military Morale for school-age draftees."

On his way out, Brett stopped at Gruber's desk and said, "I've left a few comments with your secretary."

"Thank you very much," Gruber said pleasantly. "I hope I haven't delayed you unnecessarily."

"Not at all. By the way, there's one item I wanted to mention personally, rather than emphasizing a minor point in a memorandum. It occurred to me that someone might misconstrue your reference to the service wife as being 'dumped on a hostile community like an unwanted barracks bag every time her husband goes overseas.' Sometimes a phrase like that can be distorted and over-emphasized."

"Do you really think people are that sensitive to such a harmless play on words?"

"I'm not talking about people; I'm talking about reporters who sometimes seize upon a phrase like that and play it up in headlines that can be very embarrassing to the government spokesman credited with coining the phrase. We've had several examples recently in the case of one Cabinet member who's now afraid to open his mouth in public."

"Very well, we'll delete the 'barracks bag' reference,

just to be on the safe side, and I'll pass your comments and suggestions along to Mr. Hale."

Brett hurried back to his office, where Eileen was proofreading the memorandum she had typed for him during his absence.

She looked up with a troubled expression as he entered. "Mr. Cable, this is almost unbelievable," she said. "I've never been so shocked by anything in my life. Does Mr. Gruber . . . know?"

"That I know?" Brett finished the question for her, and she nodded.

"I'm not sure yet," he said. "He wanted my comments on a speech he'd written for Undersecretary Hale to make at the CCC Conference."

"Was it . . . ?"

"Loaded? Well, even if it was, I'd have been foolish to say so. All I can do is to mention it in my daily work report to Secretary Wells, without any comments, as a service performed at the request of Undersecretary Hale's Special Assistant. But tomorrow I'll dictate a memorandum for Mr. Wells, giving him my personal and private opinions about it. Now, Eileen, I've already kept you overtime, and I don't want you to miss the last bus and have to take a taxi home after dark."

"But you still have two reports you'll need typed; Colonel Howe asked me to remind you that they're due tomorrow morning."

"Don't worry, I can type them myself in two words, 'Rejection Recommended'—with these exhibits, which speak for themselves. And whatever you do, don't discuss this with anyone or indicate in any way that you suspect anything wrong, understand?"

"Oh, yes. It's too awful even to think about!"

"Good. Just put it out of your mind until I can report to Secretary Wells. Once he has all the facts, there'll be nothing to worry about. Good night, now, and don't miss that bus."

"Good night, Mr. Cable, and thank you."

Eileen hurried out, and Brett sat down at the typewriter. In a short time he had completed a memorandum to Secretary Wells, recommending disapproval of the Air Force's request for an endorsement of *Jet Bomber* and the request of *Our Armed Forces* for an aritcle on "The Problems of Military Morale." To this memorandum he attached the analysis of inter-connecting relationships which he had dictated to Eileen. He then placed the completed report in his safe and had just finished locking it when Colonel Howe entered the room.

"Hello, Matt," Brett said. "I've just completed those reports you asked about, and I'll be all set for Secretary Hale tomorrow morning."

Matt looked at Brett with a peculiar expression. "Are you sure?" he asked.

Brett paused. "Yes, they're here in my safe. If you want to see them now . . ."

"No, they can wait. Do you mind if I close the door?"

"Not at all, Matt. Why, what's up?"

Matt closed the door and sat down in the chair beside Brett's desk. "Brett," he said, "I've got some bad news for you. Someone has told Undersecretary Hale that you said his speech is 'pink.' He's hopping mad, and has complained to Mr. Wells. I was with Mr. Wells when Hale stormed in and demanded your scalp. Mr. Wells was flabbergasted at first, then extremely upset. He left early, after telling me he wants to see you the first thing tomorrow morning. What on earth is this all about, any-how?"

Brett sighed wearily. "It means that I didn't move quite fast enough, for one thing. Matt, if I'd told you an hour ago what this is all about, it might have made sense to you. But somebody beat me to the punch, and now it's too late. Denials won't help, when I don't know all that's been said and who said it. But I've never in my life referred to anyone or anything as 'pink.' That's a libel-ous term and a sure ticket to limbo for any government employee who applies it to any public figure without ab-solute proof acceptable in a court of law—any cub re-porter could tell you that. And as for Secretary Hale, I've never seen even a picture of the man. I don't even know what he looks like."

Matt looked bewildered. "I got the impression you'd put it on paper. When Hale blew in he was waving a memorandum he said you'd written about his speech. And I distinctly heard him say you'd *said* it was pink."

"Please believe me, Matt, I've never used the word, and the comments I dictated to Gruber's secretary didn't even imply that the speech was anything except inappro-priate for the audience concerned. I did tell Gruber per-sonally that I thought one sequence in the speech was inappropriate, but I didn't even say it was in poor taste, which I thought it was."

"Brett, I do believe you. And I'll go in with you to-morrow and help you explain this thing to Mr. Wells."

"Thanks, Matt. But it's too late. Tomorrow morning I'll be called in and told that my employment is being terminated—or, in plain English, that I'm being fired."

Matt's eyes flashed indignantly. "On what grounds? If

you haven't done anything wrong, how can they fire you?"

"It's all very simple," Brett said laconically. "You see, I'm now a 'controversial figure'—which ends my usefulness as a government employee—particularly in the field of public relations where my duties involve contacts with the press. Anyone in my field must never exhibit strong feelings of his own—especially on any subject having political implications. And the term I'm charged with using has political implications far beyond any of the worst epithets which are tossed back and forth during the heat of an election campaign. You can call a man a liar, a cheat, or a crook and get away with it if you can back it up. But if you call him 'pink' you're implying that he's working with the enemy—which is a mighty hard thing to prove about a high-level public figure whose appointment was signed by the President of the United States."

Matt looked startled. "You don't mean . . . golly, we *did* have one, in the Treasury Department—during World War Two!"

"No, I don't believe there's one in the Department of Defense—at least not at that level. But I'm sure about one thing, Matt: someone in the Pentagon has tried to discredit me, and it's ten to one that he's succeeded."

"But *why,* Brett? Why would *anyone* . . ."

"He's afraid I know too much."

"About what?"

"About what I'm going to try to get Secretary Wells to understand when I see him tomorrow morning."

CHAPTER FOURTEEN

Controversial Figure

Promptly at eight o'clock the next morning Colonel Howe came into Brett's office and said, "Mr. Wells asked me to tell you to come into his office. He wants to see you alone. Good luck, Brett."

"Thanks, Matt," Brett said.

He walked into the Secretary's office, and Matt closed the door behind him.

Secretary Wells, usually smiling and relaxed, was grim-faced and angry. "Sit down!" he said, glaring at Brett. "You've been raising hell all over the Pentagon in my absence, and it's going to stop right now! I've got trouble enough, without having it generated by my own staff!"

"Mr. Secretary," Brett said quietly, "I understand that Undersecretary Hale told you I said the speech written for him was 'pink.' Is that what you are referring to?"

Wells looked surprised. "Yes, it is. And it places me in a very embarrassing position. You know that I report directly to Stacy Hale, and that he's one of my closest friends. I simply will not tolerate such conduct by a member of my own staff. And I'd never have believed that you, of all people, would even think of saying such a thing."

"Mr. Secretary," Brett said slowly, "please let me make

this clear: I did *not* say, or even imply, that Undersecretary Hale's speech was 'pink.' I did write a short comment, at the request of his Special Assistant, Mr. Gruber. Here's a transcript of what I dictated to Gruber's secretary." He handed Wells a sheet of paper copied from his notes. "And I did tell Mr. Gruber that his reference to the service wife as 'a barracks bag' might backfire and embarrass Undersecretary Hale."

Wells was taken aback. As he read the transcript, his air of righteous indignation faded. "Well, there's certainly nothing wrong with this. And I must say that I agree with it. But that's not all. I've had complaints about you from all over the Pentagon—from the Air Force, the Navy, from MID and OPR—even from the Pentagon Publications Section, clear down in the sub-basement, of all places. You had no business going down there, and why you had to go stirring them up is simply beyond me."

"May I ask what kind of complaints have been made about me?"

"Well, among other things, I'm informed that you're uncooperative about deadlines—you've blocked the Air Force twice on an important project they've asked me to endorse—that you've made unreasonable demands on all of the service Public Relations offices, that you've criticized MID's efficiency, and that you've been snooping through the files not only down in OPR but clear over in the Old Navy Building, where you even threatened to kick in the door unless you got what you wanted."

Brett smiled, unable to suppress a soft chuckle as he recalled Colonel Howe's impatience when they had been refused access to the room where the Navy Combat Art

Section's best paintings were hidden, and how quickly the door had been opened for them after Colonel Howe had ordered the Marine Corporal to kick it in unless it was unlocked immediately.

"Mr. Secretary," Brett said, "I suggest that you ask Colonel Howe about the latter incident. And as for the Pentagon Publications Section, I've never been below the first floor of this building, and I didn't even know it had a sub-basement until yesterday. And Major Joe Tuttle of OPR can tell you that I've always gone through authorized channels in referring to their files. The only criticism I've made regarding MID—if it can be called a criticism —was to ask if they had a copy of a well-known reference book that every intelligence agency should have."

Wells listened intently as Brett continued: "As for blocking the Air Force on their request for your endorsement, I don't think you'll want to endorse their project when you have all the facts. And the only way I could get those facts for you was by referring to back issues of the service Public Relations Newsletters—which I requested to have delivered by officer messenger, if necessary, from each of the service Public Relations offices—because of the time element involved. If that's what they mean by 'unreasonable demands,' then I've been unreasonable. But I urge you, Mr. Secretary, to reserve judgment until you've read a report on this entire situation which I've almost completed."

Wells tapped his fingers on his desk and stared out of the window before replying. "What do you mean by 'this entire situation,' Brett?"

"My report will make that clear. In its present form it isn't completed staff work. But it covers a serious situation which adversely affects everything you hope to accomplish in your present assignment, and it will be accompanied by documentary evidence to back it up."

"Very well. I'll give you until six o'clock this evening to submit your report. But in the meantime, you're not to leave your office for the rest of the day or telephone anyone else in the pentagon. Is that understood?"

"Yes, Mr. Secretary."

"All right, Brett. I'm sorry this had to come up, and I hope we can straighten it out."

"Thank you, Mr. Secretary."

When Brett returned to his office, Eileen said, "Major Tuttle has telephoned several times. He wants you to call him right away."

"Please call him back," Brett said, "and tell him I'm under the gun on a deadline and can't leave the office for the rest of the day. And I'll want you to bring me a lunch tray today, Eileen. I'll be working late on a special report for Secretary Hale. And if anyone else calls—except my wife—just say that I've asked you to take any messages."

"Yes, Mr. Cable," Eileen said. She dialed a number and asked, "Is Major Tuttle there?"

A voice from the doorway answered, "No, he's right here," and Major Joe Tuttle strode into the room. "Excuse me for barging in like this, Brett," he said, "but I've *got* to see you—right away. Let's go get some coffee." He motioned to the doorway.

"I'm sorry, Tutt," Brett said quietly, "but I can't leave the office just now."

"Then maybe your secretary could get us some coffee," Major Tuttle suggested. He looked expectantly at Eileen, who looked inquiringly at Brett.

Brett glanced at Eileen, who sat tense and silent at her

desk. When she made no move to go, Major Tuttle slowly and deliberately removed his beribboned battle jacket, then his necktie, and began unbuttoning his shirt. No one spoke, and the sudden silence was charged with tension.

Neatly and carefully, Major Tuttle laid his jacket and shirt over the back of a chair and unbuckled his belt. Eileen stared at him, gripping the edge of her desk until her knuckles grew white.

Looking steadily at Eileen, Major Tuttle said casually, "Brett, I'm about to show you some very artistic tattooing on a most unusual area of the male epidermis. I don't think anyone would object if your secretary went to the powder room for a few minutes, but if she'd rather stay here . . ."

Eileen hesitated for a moment, and Major Tuttle peeled off his undershirt, baring a chest so hairy that it would have made an orangoutang envious. Eileen closed her eyes and swayed slightly, then stood up shakily and hurried out of the room, closing the door behind her.

Both men rocked with silent laughter, while Major Tuttle donned the clothing he had removed.

"Tutt, you dog, I thought she was going to faint!" Brett said, trying to smother his amusement.

"I was hoping she would," Tutt admitted, grinning. "At least we'd have had time to talk, before throwing water on her." His face grew serious. "Now, before she comes back: Brett, what the devil is going on around here?"

"How do you mean, Tutt?"

"Obviously you've been told not to leave your office, and your secretary has instructions to report everything you do and not to leave you alone with anyone. And I've been called on the carpet by practically everybody—the Director of OPR, the Undersecretary of Defense, two MID Inspectors, and the Commandant of the Marine Corps. They won't tell me anything, but they all grilled me about *you*."

"I'd surmised as much," Brett said, "and I'm glad you came to me, Tutt, or I'd have thought you were mixed up in this thing. What did they want to know about me?"

"They all asked about the same things—what you'd asked for in OPR or in the Pentagon. I got the impression they were trying to hang a security violation on you, until I got my orders."

"Your orders!" Brett repeated.

"That's right. Here they are—dispatch orders to extended duty as a special observer with the Navy's Antarctic Expedition—two years at the South Pole, which is just about as far from home and any other Marine Corps activity as they can send me."

Brett stared at the mimeographed message. "Tutt, I can't tell you how sorry I am—and how much I appreciate the way you've stuck your neck out to come in and tell me. But you'd better leave now—before you're found in my office."

"Why? What else can they do to me—worse than they've already done? And it's the least I could do, after the way you saved *my* neck over Rabaul. But I'd feel a lot easier about everything, Brett, if I only knew it was worth it." He looked in Brett's eyes searchingly. "Just tell me one thing, if you can—and don't answer if you don't want to. I hate to ask you this, but . . ."

"Go ahead, Tutt."

"Brett, you're still on our side, aren't you?"

"Yes, Tutt. I swear I am, by all that's holy. The only

reason I'm in the dog-house is that I know too much about somebody who's *not* on our side—and I'm not sure yet just who it is—right here in the Pentagon."

Tutt's eyes flashed. "The dirty buzzards! So that's it! No wonder they're trying to cut you off. Well, I might have known you'd never get mixed up in anything except a free-for-all, with no holds barred."

"This one is going to be rough. Your orders are the tip-off: they're shipping you out just in case *you* know too much—and so you won't be around to back me up. You're my best witness—the only one who can prove that my contacts with OPR were through official channels and in connection with my assigned duties. Have I ever bothered you with any unreasonable demands for service, or snooped through any files in OPR without clearing first with you or with the section concerned?"

"Lordee, no! Is *that* all you're charged with?"

"No—something far worse: I'm supposed to have said that a statement prepared for a high Pentagon official was 'pink.' And you've been in public relations long enough to know what *that* means."

"Who—ee!" Tutt said. "They're *really* after you, aren't they? Brett, please forgive me for asking you what I did—but now that I know who the opposition is, and what kind of ammo they're using, I can sleep at night—no matter where they send me—so long as I know it's a real fight—and what a Donnybrook *this* is going to be! Gosh, how I'd love to be in on it!"

"You're in it up to your ears, Tutt. Don't turn your back on anyone you can't trust, from now on."

"The same goes for you, Brett. You're obviously a high-priority target: no one ever launched a co-ordinated air attack just to sink a row-boat. Watch your step—and don't take any chances." He grabbed Brett's hand and pumped it vigorously. "So long, Brett, and good luck to you," he said, as his eyes filled. "I'm proud to know you."

"Thanks, Tutt," Brett said, "and may the good Lord be with you and bring you back safely."

As soon as Major Tuttle left the office, Eileen returned. Brett looked up as she entered, but she avoided his gaze and went straight to her desk, where she began typing. Brett walked over to her desk and saw that she was merely copying from the front page of a three-day-old newspaper. She looked up at him in embarrassment.

He looked at her with a kindly smile and said, "Eileen, you don't have to pretend to be busy. I know that you're no longer working for me, and I know why you have to stay here and go through the motions. And I don't mind; you've got no other choice. So please relax, and I'll make this as easy for you as I possibly can."

Eileen's eyes flooded with tears. She buried her face in her arms on her desk and wept silently but uncontrollably.

Brett patted her shoulder reassuringly and said,. "Don't worry. Everything will be all right after Secretary Wells reads the report I'm working on. And now I've got to get busy on it."

He returned to his own desk and began typing his report. In addition to the five carbon copies required by Pentagon procedure, he made two extra copies. After he had typed steadily for nearly an hour, Eileen came over to his desk. Her eyes were red and her face swollen from weeping.

"Mr. Cable," she said, "I'm going to the Dispensary. Please call me there if anyone asks for me."

"Can you make it alone?"

"Yes, I'll be all right. And thank you for being so . . . so understanding."

She hurried out, and Brett continued with his report, describing in detail the working relationships between the Public Relations Newsletters of the Armed Services and the publications issued by the Office of Public Relations of the Department of Defense.

Writing clearly and dispassionately, he pointed out that articles by servicemen published in magazines produced by Dawn Publications had been evaluated as subversive both by DSI and MID, whose recommendations for corrective action had been rejected by the Director of the Office of Public Relations of the Department of Defense. Step by step, he showed how official publications of the Armed Services and the Department of Defense had parroted *Our Armed Forces* Magazine's endorsements of these same articles and of two motion pictures produced with service cooperation from books written by Irving Solomen. He then traced Solomen's role as the author of the pageant on which the Pastor-Chaplain program of the Civilian Council of Churches was based—a pageant labeled subversive by DSI. He added that Solomen was a member of two organizations listed by the Attorney General as Communist fronts, and was also the subject of a GBS EYES ONLY report in the espionage category.

As objectively as possible, Brett described the active co-operation of the Armed Services and the Department of Defense in the production of sixteen motion pictures endorsed by official publications for service personnel. He included a short summary of the anti-morale aspects of each film, noting that all were endorsed by *Our Armed Forces*. This magazine, he showed, not only had endorsed all of the subversive magazines published by Dawn Publications, but also contained anti-military stories, features, and articles which he listed in a carefully tabulated cross-index of items from several issues. In addition to these copies of *Our Armed Forces,* Brett submitted a total of twenty-eight exhibits containing evidence which backed up his statements. Nowhere in his report was anyone in the Armed Services or in the Pentagon mentioned by name; wherever such references were necessary, as in the case of Fred Gruber, the person involved was identified only by his title—in Gruber's case, as Special Assistant to the Undersecretary of Defense for Industrial Mobilization.

Brett was half-way through his report when Eileen brought his lunch in on a tray. She looked pale and unsteady.

"How are you feeling?" Brett asked.

"Not too well," she replied. "If you don't mind, I think I'll go back to the Dispensary."

"I think you'd better do that. Everything's quiet—no phone calls, and no more hairy-chested visitors."

Eileen managed a weak smile, and left the room. At five o'clock she telephoned Brett that she was going home directly from the Dispensary.

When Brett finished his report half an hour later, it was completed staff work, summarized in a one-page brief which clearly outlined the situation and recommended an investigation by the Inspector General. He placed the original and five carbon copies in a folder on top of his tabulated exhibits. He then sealed the two extra carbon copies of the report in an envelope, wrote his name across it, and marked it "Personal and Confidential." Using gummed tape, he fastened this envelope to the bottom of his desk drawer, so that no one could see it without crawling under the desk.

Just as the hands on the electric clock on his wall indicated six o'clock, Brett's telephone rang. As he expected, it was Secretary Wells, who said, "You can come in now."

As Brett walked in with his report and its accompanying exhibits, Wells looked up and said dubiously, "That's a rather forbidding stack of paper you're carrying, Brett. I hope you don't expect me to wade through all of *that.*"

"No, Mr. Secretary," Brett said. "These are only the items I've listed as exhibits, and they're all tabbed for ready reference. Here's the report itself, with a one-page brief."

He handed the folder to Wells, who read the brief and scanned part of the report with an air of obvious impatience, skipping several pages as he did so. At one point he smiled and remarked, "How incredible!"

Wells laid the report aside with an expression of tolerant amusement. "Brett, surely you didn't dream up all this nonsense yourself, did you? I hope you don't expect me to take this thing seriously."

"Yes, Mr. Secretary, I do. If you'll look through these exhibits, you'll see that they bear out the report."

Wells glanced through a few of the twenty-eight items of evidence laid out before him, selecting magazines at random and ignoring the official publications entirely. "Yes," he said casually, "I used to read this kind of trash when I was a boy. I suppose all kids do. But to try to hook it up with some sort of a Communist conspiracy . . . well, you're just seeing things in dark corners."

Wells paused and leaned back in his chair. Placing his fingertips together, he continued: "That doesn't alter the fact that you've become a controversial figure—so far as this office is concerned—which ends your usefulness to me. I'm sorry about this, Brett, but you'll have to go. Of course you'll have three or four weeks to look around for something else before submitting your resignation . . ."

Brett interrupted quietly but firmly. "Excuse me, Mr. Secretary, but I'm not going to resign without first hearing the charges directly from the persons who made them, and until I've had an opportunity to face my accusers—which is the right even of anyone accused of being a security risk."

Obviously Wells was unprepared for such an answer, which placed him immediately on the defensive. "Come, now, don't jump at conclusions. This is no question of security violations, incompetence, or disloyalty, I can assure you. And I'm very grateful to you for your assistance and your devotion to duty. But frankly, Brett, this matter is now out of my hands, and it will be impossible for me to retain you as a member of my staff."

"I see," Brett said. "In that case, let me suggest a possible alternative for both of us: if you'll agree to let me look for a billet somewhere else in the Department of Defense—in some other activity under your jurisdiction and under the supervision of someone acceptable to you—while an investigation of this situation is made by the Inspector General, then I will agree to waive the right to face my anonymous accusers. And I'll resign if the Inspector General's investigation doesn't completely bear out my report of active participation by Department of Defense personnel in anti-morale activities."

Wells hesitated only long enough to appraise the depth of Brett's determination. "All right, Brett," he said resignedly. "But you've got to terminate this one-man crusade of yours. And from now on, you're not to contact any other Department of Defense Activity without my personal approval. Where do you propose to look first for another billet?"

Brett looked at Wells calculatingly. "I don't know, Mr. Secretary. Where would you suggest?"

"I'll have to give that some thought. You've already stepped on so many toes that a lot of doors will be closed to you. Let me see—how about Military Personnel? I can arrange an appointment with the Director, and they issue several publications which could make good use of your talents. Think it over, and let me know."

Wells picked up the report on his desk. "Now, about this report of yours. In view of its extremely sensitive nature, I'm going to label it *Security Information* and classify it EYES ONLY. Burn any notes you used in preparing it, and don't discuss it with anyone."

While he talked, Wells gradually had resumed his friendly manner, and now he suddenly changed the subject. "By the way," he said. "Whatever became of that statement I gave you on the roles and missions of the Department of Defense? Will it require any major revisions?"

"No, Mr. Secretary. It covers the subject very well. I can have it ready for processing within an hour."

"Never mind. It's getting late, and I've got a dinner appointment. Let's both call it a day, and you can give it to me tomorrow. Good night, Brett," he said, cordially.

"Good night, Mr. Secretary," Brett said. He returned to his office and sat down at his desk, resting his chin on his hands while he thought through his next move. After a few moments his mind was made up. Reaching under his desk, he detached the envelope he had taped to the bottom of the desk drawer. He then unbuttoned the front of his shirt and slipped the envelope under his arm, where its bulk would be inconspicuous beneath his shirt and jacket. He then left the Pentagon by the River Entrance, walked rapidly to his car, and drove off into the night.

CHAPTER FIFTEEN

Max Escotti, Undercover Informer

By the time Brett reached home, it was nearly eight o'clock. His family had already eaten, but Jane had saved him a plate of hot food which he ate silently and reflectively.

While he was eating, the telephone rang, and Jane took the call.

"It's for you, Brett," she said. "Someone's calling you from New York."

Brett went to the telephone, and a man's voice with a feminine lisp said, "Hello, Mister Cable. You've got a very pretty wife, dear, and very lovely children. It would be just too bad if something happened to them. And if you want to stay healthy yourself, you'd better quit messing around with things that are none of your business. I'm sure you know what I mean, dear!"

There was a pause, and Brett heard two metallic clicks —the unmistakable sound of a revolver being cocked. Before he could reply, his caller had hung up.

Brett turned to Jane, his face livid with cold anger.

"Brett, what's wrong?" she asked fearfully. "Who was it?"

"Someone who wouldn't give his name—the lowest type of yellow dog there is! Jane, have you had any other anonymous calls?"

"No, darling, why?"

"If you do, hang up immediately, and pay no attention to whatever you may hear. And don't talk to anyone who doesn't identify himself first."

"I won't, Brett, but why? What is it? I've never seen you so angry."

"I'll explain later. But first I've got to see Gib Morrison. I'm going over to his house right away."

"But, your dinner—you've eaten hardly anything!"

"I'll get a sandwich later. And I'll explain everything when I come home. Now, don't worry, darling. I'll call you when I get to Gib's, and again before I start home." He dialed Gib's number. "Hello, Gib? This is Brett Cable. If you're going to be home this evening, I'd like to see you on an urgent matter . . . Thanks, I'll be right over."

Brett drove by a devious route to the apartment house where Gib lived, in order to make sure that he was not being followed.

Gib listened gravely while Brett outlined the situation and his meeting with Secretary Wells.

"Do you think Wells is in on this?" Gib asked.

"No, he's caught in the middle. Someone's obviously put pressure on him from above. He said frankly that my case was now out of his hands—in other words, that someone senior to him had told him I'd have to resign."

"That's your ace in the hole, Brett. They can't fire you without a hearing—which they obviously don't want. So they tried to bluff you into resigning, on the grounds that you'd become a 'controversial figure'—which is a well-known technique used only as a last resort to get rid of someone whose presence is embarrassing but whose record is clean."

"I realize that, Gib. But Wells also made it pretty clear that he'll take steps to insure that even if I stay on, my next assignment will seal me off from any opportunity to revive the case—he's already suggested a billet in Military Personnel."

"Don't take it, Brett. They'd just let you sit there and die on the vine, probably in some out-of-the-way annex where you'd be buried in paper-work."

"I know. Remember Joe Tuttle, in our old squadron? Well, he was my primary contact in OPR—and he's just received dispatch orders for duty at the South Pole."

"What!" Gib exclaimed. "Then there must be a cell operating right in the Pentagon—and something's obviously rotten in OPR."

"It looks that way. Anyone who reads the report I left with Wells would come to the same conclusion. But I'm afraid my report will never leave his office."

"You really think he'll sit on it?"

"He's already said he doesn't believe it, and that he's going to label it *Security Information* and classify it EYES ONLY. That will reduce it to a single copy which must be transmitted by hand via the chair of command. Remember, Wells has the authority to act on my recommendation or to reject it. And he'll think twice before showing a report to Undersecretary Hale—his immediate superior and closest friend—which shows that one of Hale's most trusted assistants is deeply involved in this mess."

"I get it now," Gib said. "And that *Security Information* tag involves heavy penalties, including imprisonment, for divulging such information to unauthorized persons—to the press, for example."

"That's right. I wouldn't dare tell you this, unless you'd been cleared for security."

"Too bad you didn't stash an extra copy of that report away somewhere, before you gave it to Wells."

"Suppose I had?" Brett said casually. "What difference would that make?"

"All the difference in the world. You could . . ." Gib paused, then grinned understandingly. "Brett, you old codger, I might have known you'd never let yourself get mouse-trapped! Then you *did* save a copy."

"Yes. More than one. On my way home this evening I stopped at a branch Post Office and sent one copy to the Inspector General and another to the Director of the Government Bureau of Security. I sent both copies by special delivery, so they'll be there by tomorrow morning."

"Good for you!" Gib said. "Let's have a drink. Now you can relax."

"Not quite yet, Gib. There's something else I want you to know. The day we found the GBS file on Solomen, I had to tell Gruber, before he'd back down on Solomen's pageant, which Gruber approved even though DSI had labeled it subversive. That night after I left the Pentagon, someone tried to run me down with a government limousine."

"Does Wells know about this?"

"No. You're the first person I've told. Even Jane doesn't know."

"Did you get his license number?"

"No, his lights were out. But he caught me out in the

open as I was walking towards my car, which was the only car left on that part of the reserved parking area. He was nearly on top of me before I realized he wasn't going to turn, and I had to hit the dirt to get out of his way."

"Why didn't you report this, Brett?"

"It's one of those things you never could prove—like my report—which Wells dismissed as 'incredible.' But that's not all. Tonight I got an anonymous telephone threat—someone who said he was calling from New York —warning me to lay off before something happened to my wife and children."

"Did you try to trace the call?"

"No. He hung up on me, and I was so damned mad I couldn't see straight. But now I know that someone's trying to shut me up, at any rate."

"Yes, and it shows that you've touched a very sensitive nerve, to generate counter-measures like you've described. These people are playing for big stakes, and they're playing for keeps. Let's go down the hall. I want you to meet a neighbor of mine who lives in this building. He's been all through this thing, and knows all the risks. His name's Max Escotti, and you've probably never heard of him."

"No, I haven't," Brett said, as they walked down the hall.

"He avoids publicity, for a very good reason: he was an undercover informer for the GBS. He joined the Communist party and served for several years in Communist cells on newspaper and magazine staffs and in Hollywood, at great personal risk. The GBS saved him, literally at the last minute, while he was being taken for a ride after someone exposed him."

Gib knocked on a door, which was opened only an inch before it was restrained by a heavy chain. The room inside was dark.

"Hello, Max," Gib said, "I've got a double-kosher friend with me."

"Oh, hello, Gib," said a voice from inside the room. The lights were switched on and the door was unlocked, and a small, swarthy man opened the door.

Gib introduced Brett to Max Escotti, who locked the door and replaced the chain.

"Max doesn't like visitors," Gib explained, "unless he knows who they are."

Max grinned and seated his visitors. He was an alert, bright-eyed little man, with quick bird-like movements.

"Max," Gib said, "our friend Brett, here, has the quaint notion that some very important publications are being utilized for subversive purposes."

"This is news?" Max laughed, waving to a wall bookcase filled to the ceiling with books, magazines, newspaper files, and scrap-books.

"Maybe it's big news," Gib said. "I don't think you have any copies of these particular publications in your files. They're issued by the Department of Defense, and they endorse anti-morale material as recommended reading for men in uniform."

Max sat up straight in his chair. "Official publications?" he asked sharply.

"Yes. Brett works in the Pentagon—for a very high official. And he's just been asked to resign."

"On what grounds?" Max asked.

"That he's become a controversial figure," Gib said.

"Who made the charges?" Max asked.

"He doesn't know, and when he refused to resign without facing his accusers, his boss backed down and agreed to let him stay."

Max snapped his fingers. "This *is* news—*big* news!" Max said, turning to Brett. "Are these publications classified?"

"No, they're unrestricted," Brett said, "but my report on the situation has been labeled EYES ONLY, and I have good reasons to believe that it'll be pigeonholed."

"How did you learn about this situation?" Max asked.

Brett described briefly the events which had led to his discovery of the relationships between *Our Armed Forces* Magazine, Dawn Publications, Sterling Productions, and the Public Relations Newsletters of the Armed Services and the Department of Defense. "When I compared each of these with the others," he said, "the pattern became obvious. But the real tip-off was their mutual endorsement of the movies produced from books written by the author of the Philadelphia pageant, Irving Solomen."

Max grimaced and ground his teeth. "The dirty *schmuck!* He and a few others like him have brought discredit upon their whole race. That's why I got into this fight: my mother was Jewish and my father Italian, and I got fed up with the way both groups were being exploited by Communism and decided to do all I could to stop it. So I joined the Party as an undercover agent of the GBS—and here we are." He paused and looked at Brett piercingly. "Mr. Cable, you look to me like a man with a conscience. Do you believe in a Supreme Being?"

"Of course," Brett said. "Why?"

"Because you'll need strength for the ordeal ahead of you—far beyond that required for anything you've ever done before. Most people literally cannot face what you've seen; their minds simply refuse to accept the facts, and it's much easier to pretend that such things just can't happen here in this country. But if a man has a conscience —which you obviously have—he can't close his eyes to a situation like this or quit when the going gets rough —and believe me, it's going to get much rougher from now on. There'll be many times when you'll wish you'd never learned what you now know, and you'll long for the days when life was serene and uncomplicated. For, once you've gone this far, there's no returning. You can either quit and pull out of this fight—and hate yourself as long as you live—or stick with it and fight with everything you've got and take the consequences—which can be very, very rough. And without faith in something beyond yourself, you'd break under the strain. Now, having said that, *my* conscience is clear. If you want me to stop at this point . . ."

"Please go on," Brett said. "I know I've only scratched the surface with what I've run across, and I'm interested in how it fits into the over-all picture."

"On the contrary," Max said, "you've torn a big hole in their undercover fabric—or at least you've shown how it can be done—with tangible evidence of something we've known for a long time but have never been able to prove: that the Communist infiltration of this country's mass information media is definitely linked with the military objectives of the Soviet Union."

"You say this situation has been known for a long time," Brett said. "Then why haven't our law enforcement agencies moved in on it?"

"Because the public has never been alerted to the true situation," Max said. "Even our professional politicians are naive when it comes to psychological warfare—they don't even know that it *is* warfare, and that we're engaged in a war that can defeat us without ever a shot being fired. The laws we're trying to apply were made for peace-time situations—not an undeclared emergency like this one. A law-abiding society like ours is a sitting duck for an enemy that knows no laws, has no religious or moral scruples, and which has already declared its intention to destroy us. What the American people and its lawmakers can't understand is that this is no longer a question of *morals* but of *national security,* involving our survival as a nation."

Max pointed to the bookshelves that lined the walls of his apartment. "See those shelves?" he said. "They're filled with examples of Communist infiltration of all of our mass information media—books, plays, cartoons, magazines, newspapers, movie and TV scripts, song lyrics, book reviews, advertisements—everything we see or hear or read. Now, how does this get by? Simply because our laws governing these media were designed to protect out *morals,* instead of our *lives.* Most of these laws were enacted long before the birth of the Communist Party. Who would have dreamed—even twenty years ago—that our own magazines and movies and comics could be used by an enemy power to destroy our ability to defend ourselves against armed attack?"

"A few weeks ago, I wouldn't have believed it," Brett admitted.

"Exactly," Max said. "And now your chief can't believe it even when he's seen the evidence. By viewing this as a *moral* problem, our lawmakers haven't even been able to eliminate the very things their laws are supposed to prevent—which is the publishing and distribution of anything lewd, lascivious, salacious, pornographic, or 'indecent.' The sale of pornographic material is a half-billion-dollar-a-year business in this country today—much of it managed and supplied by Communist agents. And why? Because the average parents can't get aroused about someone else's morals, unless they catch someone selling their own kids filthy pictures—and then it's hushed up as a 'morals case.' As a result, we make no attempt to suppress material filled with violence, brutality, sadism, masochism, and disrespect for law and authority—which are the stock-in-trade of the anti-morale operators."

"Gib tells me you served in Communist cells," Brett said. "How long ago was that?"

"Nearly three years—before their present program swung into high gear. What you've told me is especially disturbing, for it indicates that they're moving directly into the military personnel area. Their basic target—as in all countries subverted by Communism—is the country's young people. Of course they're always working to discredit the Congressional investigating committees, to end the use of informer witnesses, to open the files of the GBS, to stir up racial conflict over the integration issue, to ban the testing of atomic weapons, to recognize Communist China and admit her to the United Nations, to end censorship, fingerprinting and wire-tapping, and to take over the labor unions."

"What is their major objective in the labor field?" Brett asked.

"To destroy American industry," Max replied. "Labor is a primary target because the Soviets view it simply as an extension of our *military* capacity—and rightly so, for our ability to produce was the deciding factor in both World Wars. Labor is the backbone of any nation's defense. That's why the Reds concentrate on the unions: they're trying to infiltrate all our vital communications and transportation agencies so thoroughly that we'd be helpless in an emergency. They hope ultimately to be able to paralyze us by calling a general strike the moment it appears that war is imminent."

"Will they get away with it?" Brett asked.

"I doubt it," Max said. "Some of the smaller unions are tainted, but no one is more anti-communist than the big American labor federations, who know that they're competing directly with about sixteen million slave workers in Soviet labor camps. America's labor leaders are speaking out against communism and all it stands for. They're also cracking down on union officials who take the Fifth Amendment for any reason. Grafters are always vulnerable to blackmail—the enemy agent's favorite weapon. Communism and corruption go hand in hand—as our labor leaders know only too well. They realize that under communism workers are only slaves."

"What is the best gauge of the Soviet military timetable?" Brett asked.

"Their activities in the area of atomic weapons—always," Max said. "That includes not only their own development programs, but their efforts to sabotage our capacity for atomic retaliation when they attack—particularly their 'peace' overtures. Just remember that one of our most prominent and respected public servants based his campaign for the Presidency of the United States on his promise to ban all further tests of atomic weapons if he was elected."

"That's like promising that the Army would cut out rifle practice," Gib said.

"And who do you suppose that Presidential candidate —backed by one of our nation's greatest political parties —selected as one of his chief speech-writers? None other than the distinguished author of *Nagasaki*—a 'documentary' treatment of our use of atomic bombs against Japan —published by a notoriously left-wing 'humor' magazine which devoted an entire issue to this single piece of anti-atomic propaganda which was straight down the Communist Party line. And this same author was not only a trustee of the Communist front which assisted in the conquest of free China, but is also an official of the American Association of Authors who are now campaigning to eliminate censorship in any form. He also supported the group of Hollywood screen writers who were jailed after they refused to testify about Communist infiltration of the movie industry. And he was still retained on the staff of a candidate for the Presidency, after the record of his long record of Communist associations had been published by one of the few Conservative columnists who are aware of how serious the situation is. Another tip-off to the gravity of the situation is the race to launch the first earth satellite. And shortly after the Kremlin announced the successful testing of an inter-continental ballistic missile, the Communists concentrated their propaganda on the military and civil defense areas—which is ominous."

"It looks pretty bad," Gib agreed. "Most of our Reservists with combat experience in World War Two or Korea are now too old to fight. Your toughest fighting man is 17 to 21; after that they start getting cautious. And if their will to fight can be destroyed before they reach draft age, they're useless in combat."

"You're right," Max said, "and that's the Communist goal: to undermine their morale by breaking down their religious beliefs and their ability to accept discipline—at home, at school, or in the Armed Services. The schools, of course, are a major target. If Johnny can't read, or spell, or add and subtract, he can never get a decent job, fly a fighter plane, or figure out which sector the enemy's mortar shells are coming from. And if his Mom doesn't want her boy to be a soldier, his sergeant will have a crybaby on his hands who'll quit under fire."

"Yes," Brett agreed, "and it's worse still if he's got a young wife who doesn't want him to get hurt or thinks he's getting a raw deal—which is the theme of just about every movie, play, television show, or book on military subjects that comes out these days. Of course there's always a happy ending, so that the Department of Defense can give it official co-operation and approval, but the poison has already done its work long before the happy ending. It's getting so bad that all you have to do to make half a million bucks these days is to write a book making fun of one of the Armed Services, which will then make its planes, ships, or troops available for the movie, stage, and television versions."

"Exactly," Max agreed. "And every time we cooperate with such a production we're obligingly helping the enemy to cut our own throats. It's all part of what's known in Communist cells as 'Operation Overload'—keeping our military personnel and equipment so occupied with unnecessary publicity projects that it reduces our combat readiness and lowers our overall defense potential. If we'd saved only half the time and money we've thrown away by cooperating with the production of movies and television programs which are actually undermining our Armed Services, we'd be five years ahead of the Soviets. But we'll keep on being suckers until one day we'll wake up with a shock to find that they're several years ahead of us in some phase of military readiness vital to our survival. Then we can look back with chagrin and shame as we realize numbly that we've contributed to our own downfall."

"What gets me," Gib said, "is why the actors themselves accept parts in such films."

"A few of them don't," Max said. "Some of the older ones whose reputations are established have formed their own companies and select their own scripts. But they still have to get their films shown, and many of the decent films never get screened, thanks to the 'block booking' device which forces most of the bigger theaters to accept several 'loaded' films for every independently-produced film they get."

"How about the actors who cooperate?" Brett asked. "How do they get hooked?"

"Blackmail—pure and simple," Max said. "That's how they hook the screen writers, who are the first to be subverted. A struggling young actor is 'frozen out' until he gets desperate or even hungry and agrees to play a 'harmless' supporting role in a loaded play or film. Once he does, he's really sold his soul to the devil, who demands regular and increasingly large payments. At first he seldom realizes that he's trapped. But each succeeding role gets pinker and more sordid, until he balks in revulsion. Then they let him have it: he's already in too deep to back out, and if he quits, he's finished. If he tries to get tough, they give him the full treatment: a private showing of the highlights of the subversive roles he's played, and a choice selection of tape recordings and infra-red photos of his most compromising amours. As a clincher, they show him a few case histories from the 'confidential' magazines. By that time, the poor sucker is willing to play the role of Stalin's second wife, unless he's prepared to call their hand with enough dough to fight a three-year defamation suit; but usually he's vulnerable to an income tax rap, or in hock up to his ears."

"But why haven't the movie producers themselves rebelled?" Brett asked.

"It's the same old story," Max said. "Most of them are as vulnerable to blackmail as the writers who grind out the scripts and the actors who play the parts. The public is bamboozled by the hoopla in the film magazines, by the gossip columnists and by the film, stage, and TV critics. The critics have to eat, too; and they soon get booby-trapped by the extra cash that rolls in whenever they plug a film, play, or book that follows the Party line. The critic is also protected by the nature of his writing: he can praise the performance, or the music, or the scenery, and close his eyes to the hidden message in the script. The old catch-words used to be 'stupendous' or 'colossal.' But controversy is still the life-blood of circulation, and any book, play, or film labeled 'controversial' is almost irresistible to the public—particularly if it's backed by a million-dollar promotional compaign. That's why Hollywood was so easy to take over. The movie producers have always been too eager to produce 'The Picture the Navy Tried to Suppress.' The poor trapped fools! They could all throw off their chains if only one of them had the guts to produce 'The Picture that Hollywood Didn't Want Filmed.' "

Max paused, then said bitterly, "I was there, and I saw it being done. And even though I was on the inside, and reporting directly to the Director of the GBS, nothing was done to stop it. The GBS reports were supposed to go directly to the President, but somebody in the White House stopped them—reports that I repeatedly risked my life to send out. So nothing was done—and that's how Hollywood was taken over by the Communists."

CHAPTER SIXTEEN

The Face of the Enemy

After showing Brett a few case histories of Communist infiltration from Hollywood to Broadway, Max said, "It occurs to me that you've barely touched on the television field. Haven't you seen this same sort of thing endlessly repeated on TV?"

"We don't have a television set," Brett said.

"What, no television?" Max asked incredulously. "How on earth have you ever escaped the one-eyed monster? Don't you have any children?"

"Yes, we have three," Brett said. "But we were out of the country for two years in an area where there was no television. When we returned we decided not to get a TV set until the children asked for it—and they haven't asked yet."

"You're lucky," Max said. "The movies are saturated, but television is even worse. They're picking up the worst of Hollywood's and Broadway's output and piping it right into the nation's living rooms. Anyone who uses TV for a baby-sitter had better take a close look at the children's hour. Even their live programs are loaded: one of the nation's foremost entertainers used his nationwide TV program for months to run down one of the Armed Services by portraying its officers as morons and its enlisted men as stupid fools who were too dumb to get out of serving a tour of military duty. His program ridiculed military service as a senseless waste of time and money, and made fun of everyone in uniform."

"Which media do you consider the most effective for getting across a hidden message?" Brett asked.

"They're all equally effective," Max said, "unless you break it down by the number of individual exposures—in which case the magazines are easily out in front, for three reasons: They are seen by more people, they get their message across silently—frequently in several forms in the same issue—and they have a 'reader-devotion' unsurpassed by any other medium. In addition, they're filled with attractive advertisements of familiar American products—automobiles, foods, kitchen appliances and other products of old and respected companies—which provide an implication of endorsement and an air of respectability. And these same big companies blindly support almost all magazines—even some which are actively undermining public confidence in their very existence. Last year the magazines took in 723 million dollars in advertising revenues alone, in addition to about 35 million dollars in sales. Circulation-wise, the magazines easily lead all media, with about 184 million copies, compared with only 55 million newspapers a day, 121 million radio sets, and 37 million household TV sets. The advertising experts claim that magazines influence our daily living habits more than any other medium."

"But how do some of the worst offenders among the magazines exist—those which carry very little advertising, but are printed on slick paper and expensively illustrated?"

"Just like the *Daily Worker*," Max said. "They're subsidized. During the past ten years nearly a dozen of our biggest and best family magazines have folded. Some of these were pushed into bankruptcy by editing so inept that it clearly must have been intentional—in some cases by known homosexuals who were obvious targets for the Communist blackmail approach which was so effective in taking over Hollywood and the show business. But in that same ten-year period only two slick-paper confession magazines have gone under, and today there are 24 of these 'girlie' magazines circulated to more than ten million impressionable young housewives and teen-age girls. And that's only one group of magazines aimed at a comparatively small target audience. Altogether, the Kremlin spends over 750 thousand dollars a year on propaganda in the U.S. alone, and a lot of it goes to the magazines which follow the Communist Party line."

"Is that why they're so touchy about censorship?" asked Brett.

"Of course," Max said. "That's why they try to limit censorship to matters which are obscene—and then defend themselves on the grounds that there is no such thing as obscenity, by citing hundreds of other books, plays, movies, and magazines which are also obscene. That issue has confused juries and judges all the way to the Supreme Court—which usually sides with those who hide behind the First Amendment—freedom of speech and of the press. Occasionally the Supreme Court will uphold a conviction in a flagrant obscenity case—usually in a split decision which lambastes the State obscenity laws as a form of 'book burning'—but those who are convicted are usually dupes or independent operators. The real Communists always take care to operate just inside the law—protected by hundred-thousand-dollar-a-year lawyers who can hopelessly confuse any jury."

"Then censorship itself is being used to discourage our law-enforcement agencies?" asked Brett.

"Precisely," Max said. "Convictions in the lower courts not only are reversed by Supreme Court decisions, but our eminent Justices maintain that the worst form of community censorship is the opinion of the majority, and that they have complete confidence in the public's ability to reject noxious material. What they don't realize is that the public is swamped by such material from all sides. Have you ever watched the movie trailers used to advertise forthcoming films? Well, those trailers aren't censored—but they frequently contain objectionable scenes which the state censors have eliminated from the films themselves—and many theaters show several of these concentrations of censored material every night—often weeks ahead of the film showing. The same technique is used in shortening old movies for televising: the worst parts are not only retained, but are overemphasized by eliminating the milder scenes."

"Tell Brett about the foreign film setup," Gib said.

"You mentioned Sterling Productions," Max said to Brett. "Well, here's how they operate overseas. In the first place, American films need not be censored if they're shown outside of the United States, and some of the stuff that's sent overseas is so anti-American it would make you vomit. But that isn't enough for Sterling Productions. They produce films in France that would shock even the Supreme Court. These films are in English, and they're produced, financed and distributed by an American film company, so that they're technically American films—

even though some of the actors are Communists and the directors are Russians. The finished product—which is always violently anti-American—is shown almost everywhere in the world except the U.S. Production costs average well over half a million dollars per film—and you can guess who supplies the money."

"This is depressing," Gib said facetiously. "Let's talk about something funny—humor, for instance."

Max continued: "Humor is just about dried up, except for some of the earlier animated film cartoons. Even the animal cartoons today are filled with mayhem and violence, with man's traditional friends among the animals cast either in the role of villain or scapegoat. Our greatest film comedian went over to the enemy years ago, while he was still in Hollywood, where he produced some heavy-handed caricatures of Big Business which are among Communism's most highly-prized anti-Capitalist films. Comic books, of course, were one of the first of all media to be taken over, until even a child could see what was going on. For a while they were policed by the Decency Code, but it's so vaguely worded and full of loopholes that all but the crudest material can easily slip through. They're a natural target, because they only cost a dime and can be printed by the millions on the cheapest of newsprint. But a dime will still buy a candy bar or a sack of peanuts—which many a healthy kid prefers to buy instead of reading matter. The obvious answer to this minor obstacle was to let Mom and Pop buy the comics—not only in the huge collections in the Sunday newspapers, but also in the slickest of our slick-paper magazines. Cartoons are one of the most effective ways to attack our basic institutions."

Max handed Brett a magazine, saying, "Here's the

latest issue of one of our most respected weekly 'family' magazines. There are cartoons on 25 pages. Now, remember that while small fry can't read, they love to look at 'funny pictures,' and to associate them with their own experiences. Of these 25 cartoons, 14 show husbands or wives—who are Mom and Pop, to the kids—as stupid, drunk, or cowardly. Four depict the inconsiderate boss—Big Business—or the arrogant rich. Three portray marriage unfavorably or children as undesirable. Only four cartoons out of the 25 could qualify as innocuous humor of the whimsical, exaggerated, or understated variety."

Brett looked at the cartoons and handed the magazine to Gib. Max looked at Brett and said, "I'm sure you know what would happen if you tried to do something about this. You'd be accused of vigilantism, called a kill-joy, and tagged as a crack-pot. The editors could always point to their anti-communist editorials, which are widely quoted. But who reads the editorials? Not the children—who are the chief target—or even teen-age Johnny, who was brought up on a diet of comics and skips every word with more than three syllables, such as 'totalitarian.' Johnny, and his sister Jennie—if she's been exposed to 'progressive' education—just look at the cartoons and the pictures, which confirm their low opinion of all grownups who represent discipline in any form."

"You paint a mighty grim picture," Brett said. "Isn't there anything that can be done to wake up this country?"

"I'm afraid not," answered Max, pessimistically. "It's gone almost too far to stop, and it's almost too big to fight. Our entertainment, informational, and educational institutions are honeycombed below the surface, where it doesn't show. The Soviets spend five times as much in this country as we spend trying to tell our story to the *whole world,* and our magazines can be confiscated and our broadcasts can be jammed—while theirs are protected by directives of the United States Supreme Court. And worst of all, most of their activities in this country haven't even been identified, as far as the general public is concerned. Only a few scattered groups and a couple of Congressional Committees have even the faintest idea how far the virus has spread, and they are targets for the most vituperative attacks that can be devised—not only by the Communist underground apparatus, but also by the Liberal press, which is aided, abetted, and financed through unlimited funds slipped in via Switzerland. It's hard to do much when you're pilloried on the front pages by some of the world's most capable cartoonists who depict you as an ape-like gangster who hounds innocent people to death, and your office is flooded with mail and telegrams protesting your Fascist, hate-mongering activities which are a disgrace to every decent American, and your wife is insulted and your children threatened, if you know what I mean."

"Yes, I do," Brett said. "An anonymous telephone call I received tonight is what brought me here."

"You're really getting in deep," Max said. "But you never could prove that you've been threatened, and you can't get anyone to believe most of this—except when they see it in its bolder and more brazen forms, like picketing the White House to protest the execution of the atomic spies. There are so many legal loop-holes that the hidden Communist or smart fellow-traveler almost never gets caught. For a while we had them on the run by joining their cells, like I did. But now they've gone underground—some of them in the highest government echelons—up to and including the Assistant Secretary level."

Brett looked startled. "Have you proof of this?" he asked Max.

"It's in the public record," Max said. "Here's the published transcript of sworn testimony before a Congressional investigating committee by a high-level Communist agent who defected and informed the GBS. This agent worked with a group so effective that an Air Force General in the Pentagon actually gave them the date of the Allied landings in Normandy four days before D-day. One of this group was an Assistant Secretary of the Treasury Department, who enabled the Soviets to steal several billion dollars from us by giving them the printing plates with which we printed the paper money used by our occupation troops after the war. When he was exposed, he had a sudden 'heart attack' and died very conveniently before the other ringleaders could be exposed. But the damage was already done: inflation ran wild, and civilians in those occupied areas died of starvation by the thousands. Western Europe nearly went Communist as a result."

"Tell Brett how Asia was taken over," Gib said.

Max took a small card from a folder and looked at it for a long moment. He held the card in his hand as he continued: "The cell in the Treasury Department was extremely effective, but its accomplishments were as nothing compared with what the Communist cell in the State Department achieved. This is a press pass issued to me while I was a card-carrying Communist and a member of a cell in the staff of one of our oldest and most respected metropolitan newspapers. It is signed by the Secretary General of the first plenary session of one of the most important international conferences ever held—the United Nations Organizational Conference in San Francisco which gave the Soviets the greatest non-military weapon they ever had: the power of veto in the Security Council of the United Nations. The man who signed that card was the brain behind the whole affair and was largely credited with the 'success' of the conference. He was given the honor of presiding at the opening session, in recognition of his untiring efforts for a world organization united in the pursuit of 'peace.' Here's a photo of the President of the United States publicly congratulating him on the speakers' platform at the opening session. Note the date on the card—April 25, 1945, nearly four months before the Japanese surrender. Yet Comrade Molotov was there, pulling all the strings personally, while the Soviets were busily taking over Eastern Europe instead of joining us for the expected invasion of Japan."

Max picked up another photograph, which showed a distinguished-looking white-haired man. "This poor dupe was the Secretary of State in 1945," Max said. "When he asked the President of the United States about Russian participation in the invasion of Japan, he was told that it was a military secret. But the young man whose signature is on this card knew—because he was America's representative on the three-man committee which drew up the Yalta agreements which allowed Russia to come into the war after our top military leaders had firmly stated that Japan was already beaten and no Russian troops would be needed. These warnings were ignored—and more than a million Soviet troops with American military equipment swarmed into Manchuria when Stalin declared war after the Japanese started putting out peace feelers. The Soviets stripped Manchuria, killed 80,000 Japanese troops after Japan had surrendered, captured 594,000 Japanese troops who rotted in Siberian slave labor camps—then went on to conquer the Chinese Nationalists with American planes, tanks and guns. Part of the Soviet army rolled half-way through Korea, where they trained the North Korean army and supplied it with arms seized from the Japanese. Communist regimes were installed in China and North Korea, and 142,000 Americans were killed or wounded by Communist troops during the Korean War. And all this never could have happened except for the smart young man in the State Department who paved the way for Russia's conquest of Asia and her entry into the UN—armed with a veto power which she has used exactly for what it was designed: to hamstring all efforts for peace and to paralyze the efforts of free nations to defend themselves."

"Then you feel that the Soviets have used their membership in the United Nations only as an instrument of aggression?" Brett asked.

"Judge for yourself," Max said. "Within six months after Japan surrendered on August 14, 1945, we demobilized, moth-balled, junked or abandoned the greatest fighting force the world has ever known, all to the tune of 'Peace, it's wonderful!' And what about our great Soviet Allies, who rushed into the fray in Asia only after the atomic bombs were dropped, and only five days before the end of World War II? Did they demobilize, or cut back their armament programs, or their territory grabs? Take a look at this map: they've made 'peace' with more than half the world's population since 1945, and they're still on the march. Yes, I'd say the young man who set up the mechanism which gave the USSR the veto power which has enslaved half of the world was one of the most successful enemy agents of all time. He even lived to tell about it—to our eternal disgrace at one of our finest old universities—and he's a free man today. I'd say also that the UN veto has been almost as useful to the Soviets as the atomic secrets they also got through the subversion of American citizens. How else could they have bloodied us and beaten us in Korea without the loss of a single Soviet soldier? Or kept us from helping France—who helped us win our independence—or smashed the Hungarians—who were giving them a royal drubbing—while we sat tongue-tied and ashamed?"

"You're right," Brett said. "It makes me boiling mad just to think about it."

"It makes me even madder to think how long it took to bring this case to court," Max said. "The man whose name is on this card enjoyed the privileges and sacred trust of high government office for nearly two years after his espionage activities had been reported—by a confessed ex-Communist—to our highest government security agency, which sent the report to the White House for action. But no action was taken until a young Senator reopened the case through a Senate Investigating Committee which blew the whole case wide open."

Max handed the card to Brett, who read the signature of the State Department's trusted architect of the United Nations, Holger Fess.

Brett stared at the card, then at the photograph of the President of the United States shaking the hand of Holger Fess, then at the map showing the areas which the Communists had over-run since 1945. He handed the card back to Max with a slight shudder which he suppressed by setting his jaw.

"There must be *some* way to alert the public," Brett said.

Max shook his head skeptically. "Nothing could do it

short of war or another Pearl Harbor," he said. "But wars are no longer declared, and we can't survive an H-Bomb Pearl Harbor. Only some major national scandal, involving the Administration itself, could shock the public out of its complacency. Something comparable to the Dreyfuss Case, for example, which shook France to its foundations and forced the whole cabinet to resign. But it's almost too late now. Once we lack the military capacity for effective retaliation—which we barely have today—they'll hit us without warning and knock us out for good."

Brett was silent and thoughtful. Max looked at him keenly for a moment and said, "You wouldn't be here unless you knew they had you boxed in after you tried to point out that something is rotten in the Pentagon. And your report and all the evidence behind it is bottled up and will probably never see the light of day. So you're the only one who knows the whole story about a situation which could be extremely embarrassing to a large number of very important and highly respected individuals. Even those who are innocently involved are going to do their best to shut you up. But if you've run across a Communist cell in the Pentagon—and this has all the earmarks of the real thing—you've got to be very careful. Otherwise you may have a 'heart attack' or an 'accident.' Stay out of public places where someone can pick a fight with you, and don't walk alone at night on dark streets. If your health is good, get it on record and let it be known. And keep in touch with someone you can trust—Gib, here, for example. Call him each night when you get home, and at least twice a day from the office. If he doesn't hear from you on schedule, he can take steps to find out why, before it's too late to help you. And if you've got a family, you'd better keep your insurance premiums paid up, because you're playing with dynamite."

"I know what you mean," Brett said, recalling the driver who had tried to run him down in the Pentagon parking lot. "Thanks for what you've told me. You've staked out the land mines, and from now on I'll watch out for booby-traps."

CHAPTER SEVENTEEN

". . . so help me God."

Shortly after Brett reached his office the next morning he was summoned by the Inspector General of the Department of Defense.

He walked across the Pentagon and was ushered through an imposing suite of offices to the Inspector General who looked up with an odd smile as Brett entered. "I've just received this report you sent me by special delivery mail, Mr. Cable," he said. "I notice that this is a carbon copy, and I presume that Secretary Hale, who is the action addressee, has the original. Is that correct?"

"Yes, sir," Brett replied.

"Mr. Cable, this card attached to your report states that it contains information affecting the security of the United States, and your forwarding summary recommends an investigation by my office."

"That's right, sir."

"Well, I cannot accept a report of this nature unless it is forwarded through official channels—in this case by Secretary Wells via the Undersecretary's office to the Secretary of Defense, who will then direct an official investigation—if it is deemed necessary."

"May I ask if you've read this report, sir?"

"Yes, and I found it very interesting. Thank you for

letting me see it," he said, handing the report back to Brett, who looked at him in shocked disbelief.

For a moment Brett waited, but the Inspector General only stared at him with a queer, fixed smile. After a tense silence Brett withdrew, carrying the report with him.

By refusing to accept the report—an unauthorized copy of a document which Secretary Wells had reduced to a single copy classified EYES ONLY—the Inspector General had placed Brett in an extremely compromising position. The postmarked envelope would show that Brett had taken a copy out of the Pentagon, and that he had disobeyed the Secretary's orders by not destroying all his notes. If found in his possession, the report and the envelope would be ample evidence to convict him of a major violation of the National Security Act. And anyone in the Inspector General's offices could challenge him as he walked through the interconnecting suite of rooms to the front entrance.

Like all high Pentagon officials, the Inspector General had a private washroom, which was situated just outside his door in the office of his military aide, a Navy Commander. As Brett reached this washroom he opened the door and stepped quickly inside.

"Just a minute . . ." the Commander protested, jumping to his feet as he saw Brett enter the washroom carrying the envelope.

Brett slammed the door and locked it behind him. Swiftly he tore the envelope and the copy of his report into small shreds, flushing them down the drain while the Commander hammered on the door. The whole action took only a few seconds.

When Brett opened the door, obviously empty-handed,

the Commander stood glaring at him in speechless frustration.

"Excuse me," Brett said calmly. "I'm sure the Inspector General wouldn't mind, in an emergency. It won't happen again, I can assure you."

He walked casually past the rest of the Inspector General's staff to the main corridor. As the door closed behind him, he exhaled with relief. In addition to the copy of his report which he had just destroyed, there was still the copy which he had mailed to the Director of the Government Bureau of Security. And the GBS—as everyone knew—was authorized to investigate security matters without disclosing the source of its information, a unique advantage which had given it a well-earned reputation for efficiency and incorruptibility.

Brett returned to his office. On his desk was a note to call Merle Dawson, the GBS liaison officer assigned to the Pentagon. The note was signed by Eileen, who was not at her desk.

Apprehensively, Brett telephoned Dawson, who said, "Mr. Cable, I've just delivered your report to the Director of Military Intelligence in the Pentagon, on orders from the Director of the GBS."

Brett was too stunned to reply, and Dawson continued: "I'm sorry we had to do this, but our Bureau and the Department of Defense have agreed that all security matters involving military personnel and Department of Defense officials are to be investigated by the security agency of the Department involved—in this case by MID."

"You mean that the GBS won't even investigate or report on this case?" Brett asked, unable to believe his ears.

"That's right. It's completely out of our jurisdiction."

"But you were the ones who put MID on the right track, with your report on Irving Solomen!" Brett protested.

"I know. But your report is concerned with a situation in the Department of Defense. Remember, our Bureau is only a reporting agency, and our operations are restricted by reciprocal agreements with the Department of Defense, the State Department, and all the other government agencies which have security operations of their own. There are five overlapping and autonomous security divisions in the Pentagon alone."

While Dawson was talking, Colonel Howe entered and handed Brett a penciled message: "Secretary Wells wants to see you right away." Brett glanced at the note, nodded in acknowledgment, and Colonel Howe left the room.

"Excuse me," Brett said over the telephone to Dawson, "but I've just been told that Secretary Wells wants to see me right away. I suppose MID has already notified him about the copy of my report which you returned."

"Look, Mr. Cable," Dawson said apologetically, "I'm sorry this had to happen, but we had no other choice. I'd have done the same thing if I'd been in your place. And our Director expressed his personal regrets that his hands were tied in this case. We all wish we could help you."

"Thanks for that," Brett said. "But now I've got to go."

"Good luck, Mr. Cable, and keep your chin up."

Brett hung up the telephone, but instead of going through the open door towards the office where Secretary Hale was waiting for him, he went out through a side door directly into one of the main corridors and down the stair-well to the floor below. Hurrying down the corridor, he went into a public telephone booth, dropped a coin in the slot, and dialed Gib Morrison's number. There was no answer. He dialed his home telephone number. Again there was no answer.

Hatless, he hurried out through the Mall Entrance towards the area where his car was parked. He stopped short as he saw two Military Policemen standing by his car. At that moment a passenger stepped out of a taxicab at the Mall Entrance.

Jumping into the taxicab, Brett waved the driver ahead. "Step on it," he said, "I've got to catch a train."

"Union Station?" the driver asked.

Brett nodded. His forehead was damp with cold perspiration. He mopped it with a handkerchief and sat back in the seat until they were well clear of the Pentagon. Soon they had crossed the Fourteenth Street Bridge and were lost in heavy traffic.

As they drove east on Constitution Avenue, Brett tapped the driver on the shoulder and said, "You can slow down now. I've already missed that train."

The driver slowed down for a traffic light, and Brett closed his eyes in silent prayer. When he looked up, the first thing he saw was the white dome of the Capitol. He stared at it for a moment, then said to the driver, "Take me to the Senate Office Building instead."

The driver shrugged his shoulders and changed course as directed.

As Brett now realized, he still had one chance left: he could legally take his case to any Congressional Committee authorized to investigate matters affecting the nation's security.

After paying the driver, Brett entered the Senate Office

Building, where he scanned the office directory. He then went to the office of Paul Jardine, Chief Counsel for the Senate Committee on National Security.

Handing his Pentagon identification card to a secretary, Brett said, "I'd like to see Mr. Jardine on an urgent matter."

The secretary glanced at Brett's card and carried it to an inside office. She reappeared almost immediately and said, "Please come in. Mr. Jardine will see you at once."

Jardine, a bald, businesslike lawyer with clear blue eyes, listened impassively as Brett described the situation briefly.

"Mr. Cable," he said, "our Committee is meeting for a routine business session in one hour. Are you willing to testify under oath about what you've just told me?"

"Of course," Brett said.

"Can you get samples of some of the publications which are involved?"

"Certainly—at any newsstand."

"All right. Get whatever you can, and meet me here an hour from now."

Leaving Jardine's office, Brett went out to the nearby Union Station, where he bought copies of more than fifty magazines which could back up his testimony, including the latest copy of *Our Armed Forces.*

When Brett returned, Jardine's secretary said, "The Committee has agreed to hear you for twenty minutes. Mr. Jardine asked you to wait here until he returns. He'll be back shortly."

As Brett waited, he recalled that some of the members of the National Security Committee had been characterized as political opportunists and right-wing extremists. He asked Jardine's secretary who would be present. She checked the agenda and said, "You'll be testifying before Senator Gunther—the Committee Chairman—and Senator Seymour and Senator Morehouse. Do you know anything about them?"

"Only what I've read in the newspapers," Brett said, a bit uneasily.

"Don't worry," she said reassuringly. "They're usually described as a bunch of wild-eyed witch-hunters by unco-operative witnesses who refuse to testify and hide behind the Fifth Amendment—but you came here voluntarily."

Jardine entered and led the way to a conference room where he introduced Brett to the three Senators, who were seated casually in leather chairs around a table. A stenographer with a stenotype machine sat waiting to record the testimony.

After swearing Brett in as a witness, Senator Gunther said, "This is a closed session. Please talk freely and informally. No part of your testimony will be made public without your permission."

"I came here only as a last resort," Brett began, "after it became obvious that no action would be taken to correct a situation which I had reported in detail to the Inspector General of the Department of Defense and to the Director of the GBS."

The Committee listened attentively, with only an occasional question, while Brett related the sequence of events which had led to his flight from the Pentagon. When he described how Secretary Wells had suggested his resignation after saying that he had become a "controversial figure," the Senators exchanged knowing glances.

After Brett had testified for twenty minutes, Jardine

asked, "Shall we proceed as scheduled, or do you want to hear more?"

"Let's cancel the agenda," the Chairman said. "I'd like to hear the whole story."

The others agreed, and asked Brett to continue. They listened intently while Brett testified for more than an hour. At noon the Chairman interrupted briefly to cancel a luncheon appointment. The usual luncheon recess was omitted, and the Senators sent out for coffee and sandwiches instead. When the food arrived, Jardine smiled and said, "I'm sorry, Mr. Cable, but you don't get any. We want to keep you talking. You and I will have lunch together after we hear the rest of your testimony."

Jardine prompted him with sympathetic, incisive questions which indicated understanding and familiarity with the interlocking pattern of activities which Brett described. Brett testified for nearly three hours, with only occasional questions from the Senators, who clearly indicated that his story was no surprise to them. At the conclusion of his testimony, during a short period of informal discussion while his exhibits were made part of the record, the Chairman remarked, "I've always said that one day the anti-anti-Communists would take over."

The other Senators nodded in agreement, and the Chairman extended his hand to Brett in a warm handclasp. "Mr. Cable, I want to thank you, in the name of the United States, for your courage in coming forward voluntarily to testify before this Committee. What you've told us here today adds several important pieces to our jigsaw puzzle. Appropriate action will be initiated on the evidence you've provided, as soon as it can be presented before the other members of our Committee in executive session."

Jardine then took Brett to lunch in the Senate snack bar, where he said, "You've been carrying the ball against some tough interference for a long time, and you've made some good yardage. Now we want you to sit on the sidelines and let us carry the ball for a while."

"Gladly," Brett said. "But before I get clipped from behind, how should I break the news to Secretary Wells?"

"Tell him frankly what you've done," Jardine said. "Let everyone involved in this thing know that you've testified before this Committee, and no one will bother you. Once they know that we know, that will be your best protection."

"How about those MP's who were waiting at my car?" Brett asked.

"Only a bluff, to keep you from leaving the Pentagon and telling your story to us or to the press," replied Jardine.

"What if I'd talked to the press?"

"You'd be sunk. They'd hang a security violation charge on you and make it stick. But the last thing they want is publicity on a case like yours. What they really wanted was to scare you into resigning and then to hold the threat of a security rap over you to keep you from talking. But they can't touch you unless they can do it legally, and you haven't done anything illegal, or disloyal to your country, in coming to us. Just remember that, and don't let them intimidate you or provoke you into anything that would make you vulnerable to any kind of legal action. They may still try to bluff you, but they can't force you to do anything except to resign after thirty days' notice. But if they do, it won't be under a cloud, and they'll acknowledge it with a polite note that will never prevent you from getting employed anywhere—except in the Department of Defense, which I doubt if you'll ever want anyway. And they won't dare to put anything in your military record—which I know is outstanding, because we made a quick check on you while you were waiting to testify, through Military Personnel and the GBS." Jardine grinned, and continued: "So don't worry about being fired—they'll never risk that, because they'd have to give reasons which they'd never dare to have challenged. Go back and face them confidently, and with your head up, because you've served your country today in a way that would make every Marine and every real American proud of you, if they could only know the true story. Unfortunately, we can't tell them, but please believe me when I say that even your combat record in the last World War is as nothing compared with the way you've fought the enemy in this one."

Brett looked at Jardine searchingly. "Is it really that bad?" he asked.

"Yes, it is, and it's rapidly getting worse. You've seen what happens to anyone who tries to expose this thing. And you're not out of the woods yet. Watch your step, and don't let anyone back you into a corner. Don't sign anything except your resignation—and then only when you're ready to submit it. If they ask you to sign anything else, or serve any legal papers on you of any kind, telephone me immediately."

"When should I notify my office that I've been here?"

"Any time you like. You can call right now on my telephone, if you want to."

Brett dialed the Pentagon, and after being told that Secretary Wells was in conference, he asked for Colonel Howe. "Hello, Matt. This is Brett Cable. Please notify Secretary Wells that I've just testified for three hours before a closed session of the Senate Committee on National Security, and that I'm on my way back to the Pentagon."

As Brett put down the receiver, for the first time that day he smiled.

"What did he say?" Jardine asked.

"He didn't say anything," Brett said, with a soft chuckle. "He just whistled."

CHAPTER EIGHTEEN

A Question of Loyalty

After leaving Jardine's office, Brett hailed a taxicab in front of the Senate Office Building and returned to the Pentagon. Eileen was not in the office, but on his desk were four telephone messages directing him to see Secretary Wells at once. He took the messages in to Colonel Howe, who looked at him as if Brett had just returned from another planet.

"Hello, Matt. I understand that Secretary Wells wants to see me," Brett said casually.

"Ho-ly jump-ing catfish!" Matt said in an awed voice. "Brett, he nearly raised the roof while you were gone. And when I told him where you'd been all day, he nearly had a conniption fit. Then he took off for Undersecretary Hale's office, and he hasn't returned."

"Did he leave any instructions for me?"

"No, but you'd better wait in your office until he returns," Matt said.

Brett went back to his office, which was ominously quiet for the rest of the day. At six o'clock Colonel Howe entered and said, "He's ready to see you now."

Secretary Wells was seated at his desk. His manner was icily formal. "Please sit down," he said as Brett entered.

Wells paused, and looked at Brett with a wary, bright-eyed expression of cautious appraisal.

"Colonel Howe gave me your message," Wells said. "Is there anything else you want to tell me?"

"Yes," Brett said. "I made two extra copies of the report I submitted to you, and mailed one copy to the Inspector General and another to the Director of the Government Bureau of Security. After both of those copies were returned, I gave the same information to the Senate Committee on Internal Security."

"Then you admit that you disclosed this information—including two unauthorized copies which you took out of the Pentagon and sent by ordinary mail—after I had specifically directed you to destroy your notes?"

"Yes, Mr. Secretary."

"Have you any explanation why you disclosed this information to a Senate investigating committee without my permission?"

"Yes, Mr. Secretary. I testified not only because I felt that it was my duty to uphold my oath of office, but also for my personal protection."

"Your personal protection?" Wells repeated. "From whom, pray tell me?"

"I'd rather not elaborate on that point," Brett said, sensing that Wells was now on the defensive.

Wells drew himself up with an air of righteous indignation. "I simply will not tolerate direct disobedience of my orders by a member of my own staff!" he cried, pounding his desk dramatically. "Such insubordination is unbelievable. If you won't obey my orders you'll have to resign, and you can submit your resignation right now!"

Recalling Jardine's advice, Brett moved at once to take the offensive. "All right, Mr. Secretary. I'll submit my resignation, but I'd like to make it effective thirty days from today—which is the customary notice. After all, you said I could have three or four weeks to look around for another job."

Wells pursed his lips thoughtfully. "So I did. All right," he said meekly. "But I want your resignation on my desk the first thing tomorrow morning. And you must desist absolutely from any further contacts other than those required by such assignments as I give you during the next thirty days. For example, I've got an important speech to deliver before a veterans' group in front of the Washington Monument. Now, here's the way I'd like you to handle it."

To Brett's amazement, Wells resumed his warm and friendly manner as if nothing had happened, and spent half an hour discussing his speech while Brett took notes.

At seven o'clock Wells yawned and said, "Let's call it a day. That'll give you enough for a starter, and we can pick it up again in the morning. Good night, Brett. I'll see you tomorrow." His tone was casual but cordial.

"Good night, Mr. Secretary," Brett said, carefully maintaining his respectful attitude. He returned to his office and typed out his resignation, to become effective in thirty days. After signing the original, he sealed it in an envelope addressed to Secretary Wells, retaining a carbon copy for his own records.

Just as Brett was about to leave the office, his telephone rang. It was the Chaplain General, who said, "We've been double-crossed on that Pastor-Chaplain Program, which starts tomorrow. I'm calling you from a church near my home, where I've just screened a film which was delivered to me this afternoon with a note from Fred Gruber directing me to substitute it for that blasted pageant. I tried to screen it in the Pentagon, but was told that all of the projection rooms were booked up. So I brought it over here and ran it off in the church basement. And no wonder they didn't want me to see it! It's even worse than the pageant. I never saw anything so brazenly subversive. How can we stop it?"

"When do you leave for Philadelphia?" Brett asked.

"Tomorrow morning at eight o'clock. I'm flying up with the Vice President, who will preside at the opening ceremonies starting at ten A.M."

"That doesn't give us much time. It's after seven now—much too late to get you another film. Can't you just lose the one Gruber sent you?"

"I'd never get away with it. Remember, I'm not only a minister, but I'm also in uniform. That's why I called you. My hands are tied."

"All right," Brett said. "I'll do my best to stop it. But say a special prayer for me, *Padre,* because this time I'm really sticking my neck out."

"God bless you. I knew you wouldn't let us down."

Brett hung up the telephone and stared out of the window at the gleaming white dome of the Capitol, which was flood-lighted in the growing darkness. After a few moments he turned back to the telephone and dialed the Public Relations Director of the National Political Committee.

"I have an urgent message for the Chairman," he said, after identifying himself. He then outlined the situation, pointing out that the Vice President's participation in a nationwide program based on a subversive film could have serious political repercussions.

"That's putting it mildly," was the answer. "Thanks for the tip. That kind of publicity would be disastrous, and we're grateful to you for helping us to prevent it."

"It's the least I could do," Brett said. "After all, it was your Committee which recommended me for this job."

After completing this call, Brett telephoned Gib Morrison and said, "Hello, Gib. I'm just leaving the office, and from now on I'll call you at least three times a day, at irregular intervals, as Max suggested. And I'm going to have my family doctor check me over and mail you a copy of his report."

"What's up, Brett?" Gib asked anxiously.

"I've had a hectic day, and tomorrow may be even more so. I'll fill you in as soon as I see you."

"Can you give me any hint?"

"Maybe. Remember the three-letter signal we used that day during the big scrap above Guadalcanal?"

"I'll never forget it. That's the day I lost my left arm. I can still hear the way you sang out on the radio, *Victor Jig Fox!*"

"That's the one. Remember what it means?"

"Of course. Say, you don't mean it's gone *that* far?"

"That's right. The fat's already in the fire. I've got to go now, Gib, and I'll call you the minute I get home."

As Brett drove up in front of his house, another car directly across the street started up and drove off rapidly in the opposite direction. Brett entered his house, locking the front door behind him. Jane noticed this, and looked at him inquiringly. After greeting the children, Brett motioned Jane to accompany him to their bedroom, where he closed the door and handed her the copy of his resignation. While she read it, Brett checked in with Gib over the telephone.

Quietly, Brett told Jane of the events which had led to his resignation, omitting only those details which would have alarmed her about his personal safety. Her eyes flashed angrily as he described the attempts which had been made to suppress his report.

"The dirty dogs!" she cried. "Hanging's too good for them! But I can't understand why a man like Secretary Wells wouldn't back you up. What's *wrong* with him, Brett?"

"He's under pressure from above. Men's loyalties sometimes take strange forms, and he's suffering from an acute case of blind loyalty to Undersecretary Hale."

"Then is Hale himself disloyal to his own country?"

"Probably not. I doubt if any of this has ever been called to his attention, or ever will be, unless the Senate Committee investigates the whole situation."

"But surely they will, won't they?"

"I don't know. They're a bi-partisan Committee, and there's a Presidential election coming up next year. And Senators are just as susceptible to political pressure as the Pentagon officials whose appointments they approve."

After eating a quick supper, Brett telephoned his family doctor and requested an emergency physical examination, for confidential reasons. The doctor told him to come to a nearby hospital, where he gave Brett a complete physical checkup, including chest X-rays and an electrocardiogram.

"You're in tip-top physical condition," the doctor told him, "and here's a certificate to that effect, with a copy for the insurance people or whoever it is who wants it."

Brett mailed a copy of the doctor's report to Gib Morrison, and telephoned Gib that he had done so.

That night as he turned out the lights, Jane said,

"Brett, have you any idea what you're going to do when you leave the Pentagon?"

"I haven't even given it a thought," he said. "We still have thirty days, darling, and a lot can happen before a month has passed. So please don't worry: 'Sufficient unto the day is the evil thereof.' "

She sighed and snuggled up to him, and in a few moments they both were asleep.

CHAPTER NINETEEN

The Trap Closes

As soon as Brett entered the Pentagon the next morning he went straight to the office of Colonel Howe, who looked at him with an expression of mingled awe and stark disbelief.

"Good morning, Matt," Brett said cheerily. "What's new?"

"*You* tell *me,*" Matt replied. "Things are happening too fast for me to catch up. I thought I'd heard everything —until the Vice President called Mr. Wells from the airport. You're really in the soup now, Brett. Mr. Wells wants to see you in his office at nine o'clock."

"Then I suppose he's also been informed of my call to the National Committee?"

"Yes, and he said it was absolutely the last straw. He says his patience is ended, now that you've again disobeyed his specific instructions, and he's reported you to Undersecretary Hale. They're together now, deciding what action to take. You're to wait in your office until Mr. Wells returns."

"All right, Matt, I'll be waiting," Brett said.

He went to his office, which was empty. At nine o'clock Matt called him on the intercom and said, "Mr. Wells is still with Undersecretary Hale. He just called and said he'll see you at ten o'clock instead."

At ten o'clock Matt called to tell Brett that the interview would be postponed until eleven thirty. At eleven thirty Matt called and said, "Mr. Wells wants to see you at one fifteen. You'll have time to get some lunch."

Brett returned from lunch at one o'clock and found a note from Matt on his desk which said, "Mr. Wells is still in conference. He'll see you at 2:45."

Brett waited calmly, slightly amused as each successive delay made it even more obvious that he was being kept waiting so that he would worry himself into a state of anxiety and tension. Instead, he applied himself to the speech-writing assignment Wells had given him, concentrating on his work to such an extent that he hardly was aware of the passage of time.

At two forty-five Colonel Howe entered. "Brett," he said apologetically, "I'm sorry about the delay, but Mr. Wells just telephoned again and said that he won't be able to see you until three thirty."

Brett looked up from his typewriter and grinned. "This is quite a chess game, Matt. I wonder what his next move will be?"

Matt shrugged his shoulders. "Search me. I've never seen Mr. Wells take so long to make up his mind—if that's what's delaying him. But I hate to see you kept waiting on the hot seat like this."

"Don't worry about that, Matt. I've got plenty of work to do. But I'll admit that my curiosity is increasing by the minute."

Matt left the office and Brett continued with his work. At three thirty Matt called over the intercom and said, "Hello, Brett. I guess they're still stacked up and flying on instruments. Here's a new E. T. A.—four thirty."

At four forty-five Matt came in and looked at Brett with a strange expression that Brett had never seen on his face before. Matt's friendly, casual manner was gone, replaced by the stiff, formal attitude of an officer carrying out an unpleasant duty. "Mr. Wells will see you now," he said glumly.

Brett looked at him questioningly, but Matt obviously did not want to speak further. Silently, he ushered Brett into the office of Secretary Wells, who was tense, pale, and haggard from loss of sleep.

This time, Brett noticed at once, Colonel Howe did not leave the room, as he invariably did unless expressly instructed to stay.

Wells led the way to three chairs around his coffee-serving table. "Please sit down," he said, and when they were seated he paused.

Wells adopted an attitude of friendly solicitation. Without any reference to Brett's actions during the preceding day, he leaned forward in his chair and said, "Brett, we want to help you. We know you've been under terrific tension lately, and that you need a rest. Heaven knows you've earned it, with all the work I've piled on you every time I've gone away. But before I accept your resignation, I want you to take a month's leave of absence on full pay —call it convalescent leave, or whatever you like—and then come back and let us know how you feel. And if you want more time, I'll do my best to help you get it. We want you to get away for a complete rest—away from the office and free from any financial worries or family problems or whatever else it is that has upset you. First off, we want you to have a complete medical checkup, and we've arranged for the Surgeon General himself to see you privately, so that even your own family won't know, if you don't want to tell them. My car is waiting, and Colonel Howe will go with you to the Surgeon General's office at the Federal Hospital, where you'll get a complete examination and whatever treatment is indicated—all at government expense."

Before replying, Brett shot an inquiring glance at Matt Howe, who sat stiffly erect with his arms folded, stony-faced and silent.

"Excuse me, Mr. Secretary," Brett said, "but I want to make it clear that I'm under no strain and that I'm not upset in any way. I feel fine, and I've just had a complete physical examination which indicates that I'm in excellent health."

Wells sat back in his chair with an expression of surprise. "By whom?" he asked. "And how long ago?"

"By my own doctor," Brett said, "less than twenty-four hours ago."

"Oh, by your *family* doctor," Wells said deprecatingly. "That isn't what I mean. We want you to undergo an *impartial* check-up by the Surgeon General, who is far more experienced than any general practitioner, I can assure you."

"I'm perfectly satisfied with my own doctor," Brett said easily, "and I have full confidence in his professional competence."

"Then you are refusing this examination which we're asking you to take?" Wells said sharply.

Brett hesitated, looking at Colonel Howe, who would be a witness to such a refusal while Brett was legally a government employee and subject to the orders of Secretary Wells.

Wells noticed Brett's hesitation and pressed his attack. "I want a yes-or-no answer, right now!" he snapped.

"Mr. Secretary," Brett said evenly, "I'll be glad to carry out any assignment you give me while I am assigned to your office, so long as it pertains to my assigned duties, but in this case it must be in writing."

"Isn't that a little unusual?" Wells asked. "Since when have you required that I submit my suggestions to you in writing?"

Brett was scrupulously respectful. "Never before, Mr. Secretary. But in this case there are certain legal aspects which I'd like to check first with the Chief Counsel of the Senate Committee on National Security."

Wells feigned surprised innocence, and his right eyelid began to twitch. "Why, of course, if you insist. But I simply cannot understand what the Committee has to do with this. Would you mind explaining?"

"Not at all, Mr. Secretary," Brett said politely. "I feel that it would be improper for me to leave my present assignment—for a month's sick leave which I'm not entitled to—without first notifying the Committtee which heard my testimony and instructed me to telephone them at once in the event of certain developments. I'll be glad to call them right now, if you want me to."

Wells' eyelid was now twitching uncontrollably. "That won't be necessary," he said quickly. "I'll dictate a letter authorizing the examination and give it to you tomorrow morning. That will be all for today. I think you'd better take the rest of the day off and go home and rest."

Brett glanced at the electric clock on the wall. It was now seven minutes to five. "Thank you, Mr. Secretary," he said, rising to leave.

On his way out of the Pentagon, Brett stopped at a public telephone booth and called Paul Jardine at the Senate Office Building.

After Brett had described his conference with Wells, Jardine said, "This is a very critical situation. I never thought they'd go that far. You've got to be extremely careful. Don't submit to any kind of examination by anyone. And don't go near the Federal Hospital under any circumstances. If you do, they'll railroad you."

Brett thanked Jardine, then telephoned Gib Morrison and told him what had developed. When Brett repeated Jardine's blunt warning, Gib was alarmed. "You'd better come right over to my apartment," he told Brett. "I want you to meet someone who can tell you the facts of life."

On his arrival Brett was met by Gib and Max Escotti, who introduced a third man.

"This is Ludwig Merkel," Max said. "He's a genuine ex-Communist—the real thing, not an undercover GBS agent like I was. He was formerly a secret police official in one of the satellite countries, and his specialty was 'deactivating' political opponents in countries which the Soviets were about to take over. He broke with the Kremlin after the Hungarian revolt, and he's now in the final stages of terminal cancer of the throat, with only a few weeks more to live."

Max looked at Merkel, a gaunt, hollow-eyed man with a metal tube protruding from a bandage around his throat. Merkel nodded, closing his eyes for a moment as if to ward off the thought of death.

"I'm explaining this in some detail," Max continued, "because his larynx has been removed, and he speaks through an artificial larynx by placing his fingers on that metal diaphragm which protrudes through an incision in his throat. His doctors have warned him to talk as little as possible, because he had a severe hemorrhage and nearly bled to death while testifying before the same Senate Committee which heard your testimony. After that, he wrote his statements out in longhand and they were read into the record. We'll use the same system now: you ask the questions, and I'll read his answers."

Merkel placed his fingers on the metal diaphragm at his throat. Speaking in a strange, metallic voice through his artificial larynx, he said to Brett, "You are in danger of something far worse than the merciful death which will overtake me very soon. Please ask, and I will tell you the truth, for I am speaking from the grave. Now I must talk no more."

They sat down around a table, and Max handed Merkel a pen and a pad of paper.

Brett looked at Merkel for a moment and then asked, "What is the danger which you say I now face?"

Merkel wrote rapidly on the note-pad and handed it to Max, who read the answer: "You know too much. Your testimony endangers people with great political power. They must silence you or discredit you as a witness—a very easy thing to do. They may have succeeded already."

"How do you mean?" Brett asked.

Max read Merkel's answer: "By questioning your mental stability. They're implying that you've had a nervous breakdown, to destroy your credibility as a witness. Testimony by a person of unsound mind is worthless, so they're building you up as a psychopathic case, to prevent the Committee from using your testimony. But that's only step one. Step two affects your personal safety."

"In what way?" Brett asked.

"Mentally disturbed people are frequently depressed

and often suicidal," Merkel wrote. "Once your soundness of mind has been questioned, no one would be very surprised if you committed suicide. Fake suicides were my specialty: my 'despondent' victims have apparently 'jumped' from high places, cut their own throats, had fatal 'accidents' by 'falling' in front of a subway train or a truck, or died from 'heart attacks.' Others apparently shot, hanged, drowned themselves, or took overdoses of barbiturates. Some of my 'holdup victims' were fatally blackjacked or knifed, and some of my more subtle assassinations were achieved by means of tiny glass fibers saturated with virus concentrations."

Brett stared at Merkel as Max read this note. Merkel continued writing without pause, and handed Max each sheet of paper as it was completed.

"Here's one that'll make your scalp crawl," Max said, reading aloud: "But the most effective and widely used method, in cases where the death of the victim would cause a scandal or an investigation, is one which involves committing the victim to a hospital for 'psychiatric therapy.' In most States, mental health legislation gives hospitals the full right to apply any treatment which their staffs may decide is necessary to assist or control the patient. Once the patient is committed, no other permission is necessary even for operations, as in ordinary illnesses.

"Disturbed or violent patients, such as those with the 'hallucination' that they are being held against their will, are given electric shock treatment, which quiets the patient and produces an anaesthetic coma. In 'special cases' the patient receives 'extra attention' while still unconscious: the surgeon inserts a special instrument called a leucotome under the patient's eyelids and drives it up into the fore-part of his brain. With a few quick sweeps back and forth, the surgeon severs the pre-frontal lobes from the rest of the brain. The operation is extremely simple, and leaves no external marks.

"The patient has no sensation afterward, and never even knows that an operation has been performed. Outwardly he appears normal, but his mind is never the same again. He becomes a docile, tractable 'zombie' without will-power or initiative. Millions of such operations were used on a whole-sale basis in Soviet and satellite countries to reduce opponents of the regime to the status of uncomplaining, obedient slave workers. This operation was particularly useful in eliminating individuals who were potential leaders of revolts against Communism, such as professors, priests and ministers, publishers, editors, and newspapermen—like our friend here, Mr. Cable."

Max paused and glanced at Brett, whose forehead glistened with perspiration.

"It sounds fantastic," Brett said, shakily. "Do such things happen here—in this country?"

Merkel nodded and handed Max another note which Max read: "Yes. More than ten thousand pre-frontal lobotomies have been performed in U.S. hospitals—including seven hundred and seventy-five in your own home State. And one surgeon—himself a former paranoid and homicidal mental patient—performed over four hundred of these operations in one State mental hospital alone. The most notorious American case in the Washington area was the operation performed on a very senior naval officer who kept insisting that the public should be told the truth about the debacle at Pearl Harbor, when the White House deliberately failed to inform the defending U.S. forces that an enemy attack was imminent. You are almost in the same predicament."

Brett mopped his brow with his handkerchief and looked at Max, who said, "I also seem to recall a very highly-placed civilian official who 'worked too hard' and had a 'nervous breakdown' and later jumped off the top of a government hospital building."

Gib placed his hand on Brett's shoulder and said, "Now you know why Paul Jardine warned you not to go near the Federal Hospital under any circumstances."

CHAPTER TWENTY

Senator Crawley's Solution

When Brett came home, Jane met him at the door. "Your brother Ben is here," she said quietly. "He's in the kitchen with the children. Just before he came, our landlord was here, and he's going to cancel our lease. He said he'd been quizzed by two MID men about you, and he was very upset. When I protested, he wouldn't even discuss it."

"He can't do that," Brett said. "It's a legal contract, and we can hold him to it."

"That's what I told him," Jane said, "but he says he'll sell the house, rather than rent it to anyone who may turn out to be a security risk. To think that they would stoop to such a thing! What can we do, Brett?"

"Not much, I'm afraid. He can sell the house out from under us, according to our lease. But he still has to give us a month's notice, in writing."

Jane silently handed him an envelope.

"So he's already served notice," Brett said. "Well, we've still got thirty days. What brings Ben here, at a time like this?"

"He's just passing through, and I've persuaded him to stay for dinner and spend the night. I've tried to act as if nothing had happened."

"Good. It's no use to worry him. He'd never understand unless I could explain the whole background of this thing, which would take me a week."

Brett went in to see Ben, who greeted him with effusive cheerfulness.

"Brett, how *are* you?" Ben said. "Golly, it's good to see you looking so well. How have you been, anyway?"

"I'm disgustingly healthy, as usual," Brett said. "What brings you to Washington?"

"Oh, I'm just on my way through," Ben said evasively. "Another business trip, to New York and Boston."

"You look tired," Brett observed. "How about a drink?"

"Thanks. I sure could use one. I've had a long day."

While Brett mixed the drinks, he saw that Ben was watching him uneasily.

"Let's sit down and relax," Brett said. He handed Ben a highball, and they sat watching each other until Brett said, "All right, Ben, quit stalling and tell me what's bothering you."

"You're a fine one to be asking *me!*" Ben retorted angrily. "Do you know what I've been doing for the past six hours? Answering questions about *you,* that's what! I flew to Washington at the urgent request of Senator Joe Crawley and I've been in his office all afternoon. And you know who *he* is, don't you?"

"Yes, Ben. He's Chairman of the Senate Committee on Pentagon Policy, he's from our old home town, he owns the biggest farm in the State, and he hunts ducks with you out of season, the old pirate."

"Don't run him down. He may be Vice President one of these days, and he's trying to help you. He called me as soon as he heard about this trouble you've stirred up, whatever it is. Brett, what's going on? I've never met so many big shots in my life—Senators, Generals, and Cabinet Members. They told me you were sick, and wanted me to sign a request for free treatment for you in a government hospital. I kept asking why I couldn't see you, but all they gave me was double-talk. I wouldn't sign anything until I saw you, and you look mighty healthy to me. What's it all about?"

"It's a long story, Ben, and a lot of it concerns classified material I can't discuss. But I'm not sick, and I don't need any kind of government hospitalization. You've got to believe that, and you've got to back me up on it."

"All right," Ben said apprehensively. "I'll buy that, but I wish you'd tell me what you've done. You've got the whole darn government in an uproar. Whatever it is, you've created more commotion and got more important people upset than a declaration of war."

"Did anyone say *what* I had done?" Brett asked.

"No, but I got the impression that you'd either tried to tear down the Pentagon, or blow it up, or something even worse. They think you're either an anarchist, or that you're stark, raving mad."

Brett smiled ruefully. "Don't believe it, Ben. They're wrong on both counts. But I am in trouble, and I need your help, now that you've been dragged into this mess. Maybe this will help you to understand what I'm up against. The reason they won't tell you what I've done is because I tried to force action on a situation they want to keep quiet."

Ben's harried expression faded. "Some sort of a scandal?" he asked.

"In a way, yes. But this is much worse. It would make

the Teapot Dome scandal look pale by comparison. This goes all the way up to the White House."

"Golly, no wonder they want it hushed up. Are you involved in it?"

"No, I uncovered it in the course of carrying out my assigned duties. But this will give you some idea of how anxious they are to shut me up: they've put pressure on my landlord to cancel our lease. Here's his notice. And they tried to bluff me into resigning, on charges they wouldn't put in writing, made by persons they wouldn't identify. And I have resigned, but on my own terms, and only for my own protection. In thirty days I'll be out of work and looking for a job."

"Thirty days? Why, they gave me the impression this was so urgent I had to fly here right away! Well, you look all right to me. I had to see you myself, and now I know you haven't changed a bit. Stand your ground, and don't let anyone give you the bum's rush. And I'll back you to the limit," Ben said angrily, "against that kind of dirty deal!"

"Thanks, Ben. I knew you would."

"And don't worry about a house," Ben continued. "You can stay at my summer place at the seashore until you find another job. It's big enough for all of you, with room to spare. And tomorrow we'll go down and face Senator Crawley together."

The next morning Brett accompanied Ben to the office of Senator Crawley, a leather-faced veteran of political infighting who looked at Brett with a beady eye and said, "Tell me, son, why are you so angry with Secretary Wells, Undersecretary Hale, the Surgeon General and everyone who's been trying to help you?"

"I'm not mad at anybody, Senator," Brett said mildly, "and I've never set eyes on Undersecretary Hale or the Surgeon General."

Senator Crawley looked skeptical. "That isn't what they tell me," he said, "and they can't all be wrong. They want to help you, before it's too late, and they're bending over backward to be fair with you. Now, why don't you do as they suggest, and take a nice long rest at the Federal Hospital? It won't cost you a cent, and you'll get the finest care there is."

"No, thank you, Senator," Brett said. "I'm not legally entitled to receive federal medical aid unless I'm on active duty and in uniform."

"Don't worry about that, son. That's a mere technicality. Now, I'll tell you what I'll do: if you'll agree to a routine examination by the Surgeon General, I'll personally go to bat for you with the Secretary of Defense and do my level best to get him to tear up that resignation of yours. How about it?"

"Thank you, Senator, but I've decided to go back to civilian life," Brett said quietly.

Senator Crawley looked at Brett calculatingly. "All right, son. Let's forget about the Federal Hospital, if that's what's bothering you. Why don't you go home with Ben—go fishing and forget all about this? A nice long rest will do you both good, and you can get a checkup at the same time, if it's indicated. Here, I'll make the reservation for you myself." He picked up the telephone, dialed the Washington National Airport, and made a reservation in Brett's name. "There you are. Sorry I couldn't get you on the same plane, but Ben can pick you up later."

"Excuse me, Senator," Brett said, "but I'm still legally on duty in the Pentagon."

"Don't worry about that, son. I'll fix that up with Secretary Wells. Now, Ben, you'd better hurry or you'll miss that plane. Your brother will be along later."

"Thank you, Senator," Ben said. "We'll always be grateful to you for this. Come on, Brett, let's go fishing!"

When they were outside, Brett said, "Ben, I'm not going. Don't you see what he's up to?"

Ben stared at him. "You mean you're not going home with me? Why not, Brett?"

"Because I'd never get there. As soon as the plane landed, a sheriff would turn me over to a couple of state hospital attendants who'd throw a big net over me and cart me off to the booby-hatch with a commitment arranged by your friend Senator Crawley. That's why he didn't want us to fly back together. As long as I stay here, they can't commit me to a mental hospital without papers signed by my wife or an adult member of my family, or unless I agree to such an examination—which I've been warned not to do. But our own state laws are different—as Senator Crawley knows. Out there, anyone can sign a commitment warrant."

Ben looked thunderstruck. "You don't mean . . ."

"Yes, that's just what I mean. They're trying to have me put away in a mental ward and shut me up for keeps."

Ben shook his head dazedly. "I just can't believe Joe Crawley would do anything as low as that, Brett."

"Don't blame him, Ben. He's under pressure from above, just like Secretary Wells. But you've got to face facts, and you've seen how they've all concentrated on trying to get me into the Federal Hospital, haven't you?"

"Yes, they're hell-bent on that, I'll agree. And they did try to convince me you were off your rocker. But *they* can't *all* be crazy, or crooked."

"No one says they are, Ben. They've just gone so far that they're afraid to back down on this, that's all. Someone's got to give ground, and they hope it'll be me."

"In that case, Brett, it's got to be you. If they're gunning for you, they'll get you—one way or another. You can't win any kind of a case, with the whole government lined up against you."

"I realize that, Ben, and I know when I'm licked. I'll go quietly, but on my own two feet. As soon as I can arrange it, I'll leave Washington, I promise you. Now, let's go to the airport. I'll drive you over."

Ben glanced at his watch. "We've got plenty of time," he said. "Let's swing by your house. I'd like to say goodbye to Jane."

Twenty minutes later, when they drove up to Brett's house, they found another car parked in front. Seated at the wheel was Brett's secretary, Eileen Emery. Her eyes were red from weeping. She looked at Brett with a tormented expression and said, "I came here just as your wife left, Mr. Cable. Senator Crawley sent for her, and she left here in a taxicab."

"Senator Crawley!" Brett exclaimed. "How long has she been gone?"

"I'm not sure. At least half an hour."

Brett stared at Ben and said, "He must have called her just before he talked to us. She's probably in his office right now."

"Let's go back and get her!" Ben said.

"We'd be too late," Brett said. "I'll call Jardine. Maybe

he can help. You wait here with Eileen." He ran up the steps and disappeared into the house. A short time later he reappeared at the front door and said slowly, "It's just as I expected. Senator Crawley is in conference and can't be disturbed. Jardine is trying to reach him now. All we can do is wait."

CHAPTER TWENTY-ONE

Eileen Confesses

As soon as Jane Cable entered his office, Senator Crawley came straight to the point.

"Please sit down, Mrs. Cable," he said unctiously. "I've asked you to come here so I can help your husband, and I need your help in order to do so. His brother Ben once did me a big favor, and I knew their father, who was a fine old gentleman. Now, do you realize that your husband is in trouble—very serious trouble?"

"Yes, Senator," Jane replied. "He's told me all about it."

"Then you're aware that he's mentally ill, of course?"

Jane's eyes flashed. "That's not true. My husband is in perfect health, mentally and physically."

Senator Crawley smiled indulgently. "You're a loyal wife, Mrs. Cable. But let's face facts. I'm not asking you to take my word on this. Would you like to hear it from the Surgeon General himself?"

Jane paled slightly. "Does he say my husband is . . . ill?"

"Definitely, Mrs. Cable. The Surgeon General personally told me—right here in this office in front of your husband's brother—that your husband's actions during the past few days show conclusively that he's a very sick man and is urgently in need of psychiatric assistance immediately. Unless he's hospitalized at once, there's no telling what he'll do next. For his own protection, I urge you to . . ."

"Excuse me, Senator," Jane interrupted. "Has the Surgeon General personally examined my husband?"

"That's beside the point. In a case like this, your husband's actions were obviously so irrational that anyone could see . . ."

Jane stood up and fixed her green eyes on Senator Crawley's eyes, only two feet from his face. With clenched fists on her hips, she stood over him with an expression so angry that he drew back in alarm.

"Now, wait a minute, Mrs. Cable . . ."

"You answer me, Senator Crawley: has the Surgeon General ever seen my husband?"

Senator Crawley flushed with obvious confusion. Just then his telephone rang, and he seized it like a man grasping at a last-minute reprieve. "Hello . . . Who? . . . All right, put him on . . . Hello, Jardine . . . Yes, she is . . . Here, Mrs. Cable, this is for you." He handed the receiver to Jane with a sigh of relief.

Jane took the receiver. "Hello, Mr. Jardine . . . No, I haven't signed anything and I'm not going to!" She glared at Senator Crawley, who cringed slightly and avoided her angry gaze. "Yes, I'll come right down, as soon as I finish talking to this . . . this . . . all right, I won't say it, but I ought to!"

She hung up the receiver and turned back to Senator Crawley, who was now shamefaced and crestfallen. "Have you anything else to say to me, Senator?" she asked.

He shook his head in silent embarrassment.

"Well, I have something to say to you, Senator," Jane

said quietly. "When I came to this country, as the wife of an American officer I didn't have to become a citizen. Many foreign-born wives of Americans never do. But I took out my first papers the day I arrived, and two years later I was proud to be sworn in as an American citizen. Nothing has given me greater pride, and I've never regretted the choice I made—until today. You were born here, Senator, and you'll never know what it means to become a citizen of another country by your own choice, as I did. You call your country 'the land of the free, and the home of the brave.' Yet today you've tried to deprive my husband of his freedom—without a trial or a chance to answer the 'brave' men who are afraid to face him. 'Sweet land of liberty!' The next time you try to sing those words from your national anthem, Senator, I hope they choke you."

Senator Crawley hung his head. Jane looked at him scornfully for a moment, then turned and strode out of his office with her shoulders back and her head high.

Paul Jardine met her at the door and introduced himself. "Your husband telephoned," he said, "and he's safe at home, for the moment. Will you please come with me? I want you to meet Senator Gunther, the Chairman of the National Security Committee."

They walked down the corridor to the office of Senator Gunther, who stood up and escorted Jane to a chair.

"It's a pleasure to meet you, Mrs. Cable," he said. "I want to congratulate you for your staunch support of your husband, who is a great patriot and a very brave man. Senator Crawley has just called me and asked me to express his personal apologies to you. I don't know what you said to him, but it's the first time I've ever heard a United States Senator weep over the telephone."

He looked at her inquiringly, but she sat silently and waited for him to continue.

"Mrs. Cable," he said, "you know that your husband's mental stability has been questioned because of his testimony before our committee. What he has disclosed is extremely important to the security of the United States—if it can be proved. But as long as his mental competence can be questioned, his testimony can also be challenged. We want to preserve him as a witness, and we need your help."

"What do you want me to do, Senator?" Jane asked.

"We want you to get your husband out of Washington as soon as possible and have him examined by a good psychiatrist—at his own request."

"We're going to leave Washington," Jane said, "but whatever my husband does after that will be entirely up to him."

"Of course. It must be absolutely of his own free will. He himself must request the examination and make the appointment with a doctor of his own choice—preferably some well-known specialist whose professional competence cannot be questioned."

"I'll tell him what you've asked," Jane said. "Is there anything else that . . . that we should know?"

"Yes, Mrs. Cable, but I'm sure your husband already knows this: he's a very lucky man to have a wife like you. Please give him my sincere congratulations."

Jane relaxed and smiled. "Thank you, Senator. You've restored some of my badly-shaken faith in this country and what it stands for."

When Jane came home, Brett met her at the door. "My secretary is here," he told Jane, "and she wants to see you.

She's just been fired, and they've given her a rough time."

He led the way to the living room where Ben was waiting with Eileen. Brett introduced Eileen, who said, "I know you'll all hate me for what I've done, but you have the right to know I'm partly responsible for what has happened." She hung her head for a moment, and then went on: "I was called in by Secretary Wells, Undersecretary Hale, the Surgeon General, and several other men. They quizzed me about your actions, Mr. Cable, in front of a tape-recorder. They wanted to know if you'd been acting strangely, and I said you had."

Jane's face hardened, and Brett stared at Eileen.

"In what way?" Brett asked. "What did you tell them?"

"I told them that you'd seemed distracted and preoccupied during the past few weeks, that you'd been spending a lot of time reading comics and smutty magazines which you kept in your office safe, and that you'd been dictating long letters addressed to yourself."

"You mean my memoranda for record, which you typed and filed for me?" Brett asked.

Eileen nodded miserably. "They also asked if you'd ever hinted that you had any enemies, or that anyone was after you, and I said that you'd given me the impression that you thought there were enemy agents in the Pentagon, and that one time I had to leave your office when one of your visitors began disrobing right in front of me."

Jane and Ben stared at Brett. He grinned reminiscently and said, "That's true. Major Joe Tuttle stripped all the way down to his hairy chest before you'd leave us alone where we could talk, after Secretary Wells had told you to report everything I said or did. Isn't that right, Eileen?"

She nodded, wiping her eyes with a damp handkerchief. Brett handed her a fresh handkerchief from his breast pocket.

After drying her tears, Eileen continued: "Then the Surgeon General asked if your parents were still alive, and I said I didn't think so, and he said, 'Then we're stuck unless we can locate his closest adult male relative,' and I told him I'd met your older brother Ben, and he said 'That's our man!' I told them where Ben lived, and they warned me not to talk to anyone about the entire matter."

Ben and Brett exchanged glances, and Eileen went on: "Yesterday Secretary Wells called me in and accused me of alerting you and your brother, and discharged me for insubordination. Then I realized what I had done, and I had to come here and tell you the whole story." She turned beseechingly to Jane. "I'm not asking you to forgive me, but I do want you to understand why I resented your husband. Suppose *you* had to sit in the same room with him day after day, and he never even looked as if he would *like* to make a pass at you? How would *you* feel?"

"I'd hate him," Jane said, smiling at Eileen for the first time.

Brett coughed and said to Eileen, "Let's forget what's past. Your part in this was only incidental, and you've actually helped me by bringing Ben here to back me up. What really stopped them was Ben's insistence on seeing me before signing a document which would have committed me to a mental ward. But what about you, Eileen? What are your plans?"

"I don't know," she said disconsolately. "I've always worked for the government, ever since I finished school, and it was a real career—but now it's finished."

"Forget your career," Brett said gently. "You ought to get married again and start raising a family of your own. Nothing else in life is worth working for."

"I know," Eileen said hopelessly, "but who would marry me now, after what I've done?"

Ben spoke up immediately. "I would, Honey, and that's a proposal. I like your attitude, and I admire your courage in coming here. Besides that, you're one of the prettiest females I've ever set eyes on!"

Eileen stared at Ben, then she blushed and stood up shakily. "I appreciate that," she said tearfully, "but I realize that it's only misplaced sympathy. Goodbye, and please try to forgive me."

"Wait a minute," Ben said hastily. "You're in no condition to drive. I'm going to drive you home, and I don't want to hear any arguments. We've managed to keep Brett out of the hospital, and we don't want you to end up in one." He took Eileen's arm and led her to the door. As they went out, he looked back at Brett and winked.

Brett and Jane spent the rest of the day packing their household effects. Late that evening Ben returned with a bottle of champagne. "Let's celebrate!" he said triumphantly. "Eileen and I are going to be married!"

CHAPTER TWENTY-TWO

The Psychiatrist

As soon as they left Washington, Brett and Jane drove with their children to Ben's house at the seashore, where they spent a relaxed week occupied mainly by fishing and swimming. Brett then telephoned Gib Morrison and asked his assistance in locating a trustworthy psychiatrist. Gib consulted Max Escotti, who arranged an appointment for Brett with Dr. Hugo Nilsson, a specialist with an international reputation.

Dr. Nilsson telephoned Brett and said, "I have a place on the seashore only an hour's drive down the coast from you. I'll be there this weekend, and I can see you on Saturday morning at ten thirty. Please bring your wife and children."

At the appointed time, Brett and his family drove up in front of Dr. Nilsson's house. Dr. Nilsson, a huge man with a shaggy white mane, was trimming his hedge as Brett arrived.

"Good morning, Mr. Cable," he said cordially. "I see you're right on time. Let's take a walk down the beach, while my wife shows your family our sea-shell collection."

When they were away from the others, Dr. Nilsson said, "Now, Mr. Cable, why have you come to see me? I've been told only that you've requested a mental examination—which in itself is extremely unusual. Have you any doubts about your own sanity?"

"No, Dr. Nilsson," Brett answered, "but that's only a minority opinion."

Dr. Nilsson smiled. "There are others, then, I take it, who believe otherwise?"

"Very strongly. They've even offered to provide me with free treatment."

"But there are others, apparently, who believe you are mentally sound—like our mutual friend Max Escotti, for instance?"

"Yes, but they're also in the minority. That's why I've come to you for an objective opinion."

"Well, now. About those who question your sanity: would you say that they were mentally unbalanced, Mr. Cable?"

"Definitely not. There's not a crackpot among them. They're all men whose judgment is highly respected. No, I'm afraid I'm the one who's out of step in this parade, Doctor."

Dr. Nilsson looked pleasantly surprised. "Well, well. This *is* an interesting case. Have these, er, friends of yours indicated where they want you to go for free treatment, and by whom?"

"Yes, Dr. Nilsson. They want me to go to the Federal Hospital in Washington, for an examination by the Surgeon General."

"What! Do these men hold public office?"

"Yes, they do. Some are very high officials of the Department of Defense, and one is a prominent United States Senator."

Dr. Nilsson looked at Brett with piercing eyes. "Mr.

Cable, have you been accused of being a security risk?"

"No, Doctor. My loyalty has never been questioned."

"Good. Because I won't take a case which provides a cloak of insanity for a criminal or a traitor. Suppose you tell me just what kind of a predicament you're in, before we go any further."

Dr. Nilsson listened intently while Brett described the situation which had led to his testimony before the National Security Commitee and his subsequent resignation. When Brett finished, the doctor said, "Please wait here. I want to talk to your wife and children." He walked rapidly back to the house, while Brett lay back on the sand and sunned himself.

Less than fifteen minutes later, Dr. Nilsson returned. He was red-faced and angry. "Please forgive me, Mr. Cable," he said, "but when I think what they've tried to do to you and your family, it makes me boiling mad. Whoever told you that you need psychiatric assistance ought to come see me himself. You're as sane as any man can be—which any doctor could tell just by talking to that wonderful wife and those fine children of yours. When a man cracks up mentally, his wife and children know it instinctively, and their reactions mirror his aberrations. Your story made sense to me, but it is so fantastic that I had to check first with your wife, to make sure I wasn't up against a psychopath hiding behind the mask of sanity. There are such cases, but they're very rare and extremely hard to detect. Such individuals have one trait in common: they are completely amoral—absolutely soulless and without conscience. But you, my friend, have a conscience that is reflected by a wife and children who adore you, and who are just about the most normal and well-adjusted people I've ever met. You're a very lucky man."

Brett's eyes moistened. "Thank you, Doctor, but I also realize that it's almost impossible for a man to prove himself sane. Isn't that true?"

"Only when his behavior deviates widely from the accepted norm of his contemporaries. But what *is* sanity? Is a doctor normal? Or a minister, or a soldier who deliberately sacrifices his own life for his friends? One man's reaction in a given situation may seem completely insane to others with different moral values—just as your own reactions in this situation have been challenged by others who view it from a different perspective and see only one facet of the evil morass you've uncovered. You're lucky to be out of it. My advice to you now is to stay out of Washington and to get away from government and from politics. Forget the whole sorry business. One man alone can't clean out Washington's Augean Stables, where corruption has been piling up for the last thirty years."

"I've already left Washington," Brett said, "and I've no desire to go back. Twenty years of government service is enough."

"Good. Quit while you're still ahead. Now, let's go back to the house. My wife is fixing a picnic lunch, and the tide's just right for swimming."

As they walked back down the beach, Brett wrote his address on a card and handed it to Dr. Nilsson. "You can send the fee for your services to this address, Doctor, and it will be forwarded to me."

"Forget the fee," Dr. Nilsson said. "There won't be any. I'll consider this my contribution to good government."

CHAPTER TWENTY-THREE

The Challenge

The following Monday morning Brett received a telephone call from a man who introduced himself as the president of an executive placement service. "Mr. Cable," he said, "Paul Jardine has highly recommended you as an experienced public relations specialist, and we have several openings in that field. Would you be willing to relocate in another city?"

"That depends on the area and the organization," Brett replied. "What areas are involved?"

"One is with an airline whose headquarters are in Miami, another is with an airplane manufacturer on the west coast, another is with a Chicago meat-packing company, and there's also an opening as Director of Public Relations for one of the biggest New York advertising agencies—but I don't think that one would interest you."

"Why not?" asked Brett.

"Well, it's one of those you-can't-win situations. We've sent several top-notch men there, and they've all given it up as hopeless. The last man who took it on has just informed us that he's resigning to avoid a nervous breakdown—and he's not the quitting type."

"Which of these jobs pays the most?"

"The New York job, naturally. Their management

can't seem to understand that their troubles emanate from the top, so they keep raising the ante each time they hire someone from outside. They're willing to go as high as fourteen thousand a year—and still the job has gone begging."

"I'd like a crack at that job," Brett said.

"Why? The Chicago job pays thirteen thousand, and you wouldn't be butting your head against a stone wall—which you'd be doing if you took on the New York assignment. Par for that course is only about six months. Why risk your professional reputation by taking on an impossible assignment?"

"Because it's a challenge. If they're flat on their backs, the only way they can go is up."

"That's true. The man who succeeds in that assignment can just about name his own ticket. But I should warn you that it'll be a long, hard grind with very little help and almost no support at the start. Are you sure you can take it?"

"I'm pretty healthy," Brett said, "and I thrive on hard work. I'd like to take on that job, on a one-year trial basis. But you can tell them my price is fifteen thousand, plus your fee and all my moving expenses."

"Well, Mr. Cable, you certainly sound confident. I don't know if they'll go that high, but I'll sound them out. Will you please send me a résumé of your background and letters of recommendation from your last three previous employers?"

"I'll be glad to. And please express my appreciation to Paul Jardine for recommending me to you."

Brett then put in a long-distance call to Washington, and soon had Colonel Howe on the wire.

"Hello, Matt," Brett said. "How are things going in the Pentagon?"

"Everything's quieted down since you left," Matt replied, "and I hope it stays that way. But how are *you* doing, Brett? I hope everything's all right with you."

"Couldn't be better. That's what I called you about. I've got a chance for a good job with a big company, and I need some letters of recommendation."

"I'll be glad to give you one any time," Matt said. "I'm sorry for what happened here, and I want you to know that if you hadn't called their bluff that day, I'd now be facing a court-martial for refusing to escort you to the Federal Hospital."

"Thanks, Matt. You were the one who tipped me off in the first place, and I'll always be grateful to you. But here's what I'm calling about: will you please ask Secretary Wells if he will send me an informal note acknowledging my resignation, with any comment he cares to make about my public relations work for him while I was his Special Assistant?"

There was a long pause before Matt replied. "Wow!" he exclaimed. "Do you know the chance you're taking, Brett? If he puts the wrong things on the record, you'll never be able to get another job anywhere—ever again."

"I realize that, Matt. But I also happen to have a pretty high regard for Secretary Wells and his integrity. He was only doing what he believed to be his duty—as he saw it. And don't forget that he was under orders, too. All I'm asking him to do is write his honest opinion of my professional competence."

"All right," Matt said dubiously. "But if anything goes wrong, it's your funeral."

"Absolutely. And please express my regrets to Secretary Wells for all the worry and inconvenience I've caused him, and give him my best wishes for success in his assignment."

"Okay, Brett. I wish I had your faith in human nature."

An hour later, Matt called back and said, "Hello, Brett. I've just been in to see the boss, and you certainly called your shots, right on target. He was sincerely glad to hear what you asked me to tell him, and he just dictated a note to you and told me to send it special delivery. Here, I'll read you what it says: 'Dear Brett: This is to acknowledge your resignation as my Special Assistant for Public Relations. You have given me great assistance in this field, particularly with the many speeches which I have had to make. I wish you every success in your new job in civilian life. Sincerely yours, J. Hardy Wells.' Now, how *about* that?"

"It's perfect, Matt. As a matter of fact, it's just about the best letter of recommendation I've ever had from anyone. Please thank Secretary Wells for me, and give my best regards to the rest of the staff."

Brett sat down and wrote a note to his brother Ben. Before mailing it, he read it to Jane: "Dear Ben: Thank you for providing us with this haven of refuge at a time when we needed it most. I'm sorry you had to be dragged into this affair, and hope you'll forget all about it and dismiss it as a bad dream.

"I've just been tipped off to a new job opportunity, and Secretary Wells has sent me a very flattering letter of endorsement. I've also had the examination which I was urged to get, and the doctor says I'm in fine shape.

"Just to reassure you, please don't worry about my going back to Washington. If I land this job it will be in

New York, and I'm leaving government service for good.

"Please forgive me for all the worry I've caused you, and let us know when you set a date for the wedding. Jane joins me in much love to you and yours."

"That's a good letter," Jane said, "and I know Ben will be glad to get it."

Early the next day Brett received Secretary Wells' letter by special delivery messenger. After showing it to Jane he left for New York, and that evening he telephoned her: "Darling, I got the job, and I've found a house on Long Island within easy commuting distance. I've already notified the moving company to start packing the things we've left in storage, and I'll be home this weekend."

Jane was deliriously happy, and after Brett had told her all the details she said, "There's a special delivery letter here from Ben. Shall I send it to you?"

"No," Brett said. "Please open it and read it to me. Ben knows I never keep any secrets from you."

"It's a long letter," Jane said, "but here goes:

'Dear Brett: I sure was glad to hear that you're leaving Washington, and I hope you get that job in New York. Get your family up there as fast as you can, dig in, and wash all that rotten bad dream you went through out of your mind. I didn't want to bring it up again, but I want to set you straight on any wrong ideas you may have about my small part in it.

'When Senator Joe Crawley telephoned me I grabbed the first plane out and flew to Washington. When I got there I was sick at heart and worried to death about you. All I'd been told was that you were sick and that I should see you as soon as possible, so you can imagine how I felt.

'When I got there I went straight to Joe Crawley's office

and found him arguing with Senator Gunther about the state of your health. It was several minutes before I realized that they were talking about your *mental* health. Then after listening to Secretary Wells for two hours and then talking to the Surgeon General I was almost a nervous wreck, thinking what I'd find when I saw you. Altogether, I listened to nine different interested parties, and by the time they finished working on me I felt that I had led nine lives in one day.

'As soon as I saw you I knew within half a minute that you were the same brother I'd always known and that you were *not* cracked. Joe Crawley had kept insisting that I see Senator Gunther, and when I did I talked to Gunther and to Paul Jardine for over an hour. Then Gunther telephoned Crawley and suggested that Crawley use his influence to get back your resignation. Crawley called back and said that the officials involved had gone home for the day and he would work on it as soon as they got back the next day. Then Gunther said not to let you go to the Federal Hospital under any conditions and to see a private doctor you could personally trust.

'Then I went back to Crawley's office and he said he could get back your resignation, but he started in all over again about your health, until I asked him if he had seen you or talked to you personally, and he admitted that he had not. That's when I urged him to see you. First it was one of those "next week" deals, but he finally agreed to see us together the next day—which he did. You apparently convinced him that you were okay, and I believe he would have put pressure on your boss to get your resignation back, but then he began urging you again to go to the Federal Hospital, and that's when I cut in and agreed that it would be better if you went home with me instead. Then he agreed and as you know, he even made the airplane reservation for you himself. Of course I was very much relieved, and when you told me you weren't coming home with me and explained why, I was flabbergasted.

'As soon as I got home I called Joe Crawley, and got a complete run-around. I tried for two days to reach him and finally caught him at home. When I asked him if he had called the Secretary of Defense about tearing up your resignation, he was very vague and said "Call me up some time." So I gave up. I still don't know what it's all about, but I do know this: that made me ineligible immediately to play ball any more in that cloak-and-dagger league, and am I glad!

'So thank Heaven you're getting out of Washington. Don't *ever* go back. Whatever it is that you know, it must be hotter than the A-bomb, judging from the efforts they've made to shut you up. So please lay off it for good, Brett, not only for your own sake but also for Jane and your children.

'Now let's forget the past, and think about the future. Eileen and I were married yesterday, in a quiet ceremony with just a few friends. She wanted it that way, and she said you'd understand. We're flying to Honolulu for our honeymoon, and I'll mail this letter when we land in San Francisco.

'God bless you all and much love from Ben.' "

Jane paused a moment. "Tell me, Brett, how did you ever dare to ask Secretary Wells for that letter of endorsement he sent you?"

"Well, I couldn't have landed this job without it," Brett replied. "But my real objective was to see how far he's willing to go to keep me quiet. Actually it was a challenge from me to him, and he knows it. He and I are still playing a game of draw poker for high stakes, and it's far from finished. My asking him for a personal letter of endorsement was like drawing one card after he'd opened and drawn three cards. He may be holding a pair of Jacks, but he knows I've got at least two pairs, or maybe even a straight or a flush. If he'd had a strong hand he'd have bet on it by denying me the letter I needed. But in effect he's now checked the bet to me, hoping I'll pass or fold."

"And what are you going to do, Brett?"

"I'm going to bet every chip I've got, darling, on you and our children and this country. No man ever held better cards than I've got, and I'm going to play them for all they're worth."

CHAPTER TWENTY-FOUR

One-Year Trial

The months passed swiftly as Brett concentrated on making good in his new assignment. Almost before he realized it, a whole year had gone by. One evening he brought home a tape-recording of a speech which he had written for delivery by the president of his advertising agency before a national conference of prominent business leaders and educators.

"I want you to listen to part of this speech," he told Jane, "and to give me your frank opinion of it."

He plugged in the tape-recorder, and a vibrant voice filled the room: "Business must recognize its responsibility to insure that the system under which it operates is understood. In order to operate effectively and healthily, business must satisfy the legitimate interest of the public in its aims, goals, and operations. If business doesn't tell its own story, continuously and effectively, it is bound to be misunderstood. Worse yet, it may find that the public has been told a far different version that is distorted and injurious. I'm not speaking now about unfair business competition here at home; our own laws can take care of that. But there is another economic system, diametrically opposed to our own, which has brazenly published its intentions to subvert, destroy, and supplant the American way of life.

"Business therefore has a responsibility to insure that the public knows and understands both the nature of the economic competition we face, and the penalties for letting it win by default. The factors in this world that work for the destruction of both ourselves and our economic system must be thoroughly understood and intelligently counteracted.

"This means that industry and business have a vital interest in education—in what is being taught to our children and in what isn't. We can be confident that right and justice are on our side in the world clash between freedom and slavery. This makes our task in education easier, because we do not need to indoctrinate our youth with beliefs that go against human reason and basic instincts. Our job in education basically is to help our young people learn to *think.* With such an opportunity, and with full information, a fair presentation and a free choice, they will come to the right conclusions. What, then, can business do to improve education? What are the needs of education that business people should work to meet? First, there is the physical need—enough school rooms, buildings, books, and other equipment to do the job which our enemies boast they are doing; and well-paid, well-trained, dedicated teachers.

"But perhaps where our greatest responsibility lies is in the area of educational content and methods of teaching. Are our children being taught to *think,* or are they being taught *what* to think? What subjects and ideas are being expounded and debated in our schools—and which ones are being ignored or overlooked? What is being taught about the kind of economics and political ideology that literally makes our way of life 'tick?' How are these things treated in the schools? This question should concern every one of us, but it should receive especially careful attention from business leaders. The freedom we enjoy and our superior standard of living derive directly from the fundamental correctness of our way of life—which means our economic system coupled with our political and religious beliefs. Ambition, inventiveness, ingenuity, creativeness, self-confidence, humaneness—all these grow out of and thrive on our way of life. If we accept and fulfill our responsibility to preserve our system—our way of life—then we preserve all these things.

"The contrast we face and the economic challenge we have accepted is a win-or-die proposition, even though it is an economic clash rather than an armed conflict. And the alternatives to victory are just as stark. Perhaps no one has expressed this more clearly than Sir Winston Churchill, in his book 'The Gathering Storm.'

"Although his words were published in 1948, about events which occurred in 1938 and 1939, they are just as significant and appropriate to business men and educators today: 'If you will not fight for the right when you can easily win without bloodshed; if you will not fight when your victory will be sure and not too costly; you may come to the moment when you will have to fight with all odds against you and only a precarious chance of survival. There may even be a worse case. You may have to fight when there is no hope of victory, because it is better to perish then to live as slaves.' "

Brett switched off the tape-recorder. "That was a studio recording which was made for broadcasting over a coast-to-coast radio network. How does it sound to you?"

"I think it's excellent. When will it be broadcast?"

"It won't be," Brett said. "That portion has been deleted from the speech and cut out of the transcript."

"You mean it's been censored?"

"Well, not exactly. One of our own people objected to it. We've got a new executive vice-president who clears all public statements before they're issued. He's a former editor of a prominent Liberal magazine, and he cut this portion from the speech I wrote for the president."

"What about the rest of the speech?"

"That's also been revised. Only the shell is left—just a bunch of pompous platitudes."

"What can you do about this, Brett? Are we going to have to go through the same old thing all over again?"

"Not this time. We've been here a year now, and I've held this job down twice as long as anyone else—just to prove that I wouldn't crack up under greater pressure than most men can withstand. For a long time I've been taking it on the chin, but now I'm ready to start counter-punching. I've written a letter to Paul Jardine, with a copy for the new chairman of the Senate Committee on National Security. But before I sign it, I want to read it to you, and if you have any objections I'll tear it up and forget the whole thing."

Brett took a letter from his brief-case and began reading:

"Dear Mr. Jardine: As you suggested, while on terminal leave last year before my resignation as a Department of Defense employee became effective, I went to a nationally known psychiatrist and asked him to evaluate my mental condition.

"You will recall that after I testified before your committee in closed session, in compliance with your instructions I informed my office that I had done so. This resulted, as you know, in a strenuous attempt to convince my family and your committee that I was mentally unbalanced: Secretary Wells and other high officials prevailed upon Senator Crawley to summon my older brother to Washington without my knowledge and attempted to obtain his assistance in sending me for treatment to the Federal Hospital, which I was not legally entitled to enter.

"I subsequently learned that the Surgeon General—whom I have never met—was present during these discussions and gave his opinion about my mental condition without ever having seen me. I have also learned that my co-workers in the Pentagon were deliberately misinformed that I had suffered a nervous breakdown, and that this rumor was spread around the Pentagon among officers with whom I served over a 20-year period. (Two U.S. Marine Corps Officers who are familiar with this entire episode have so informed me.)

"Again let me emphasize this: no one in the Department of Defense ever challenged the truth of my statements or the validity of the supporting evidence I left with your committee. No one yet has ever dared to say 'it's not true.' Thus this all-out attempt—not to refute my testimony but to discredit me as a witness—speaks for itself; no one has ever wasted a battleship's fire-power just to sink a rowboat. All they would have had to do, if my charges had been untrue, would be to say 'you're a liar and we can prove it'—and then to fire me—which they didn't dare.

"When I asked the psychiatrist for an appointment, he asked me to bring my wife and children along with me to his country home during the examination. He asked me why I had come to see him, and I briefly outlined the situation without identifying any of the principals who were involved. He then questioned me about my personal and family life, and after talking privately with my wife he told me 'whoever told you that you need psychiatric assistance ought to come see me himself.' He and his wife then took us off on a beach picnic the rest of the day, and when I asked about his fee he told me 'there won't be any. I'll consider this my contribution to good government.'

"But this wasn't enough. I wanted the Pentagon's endorsement of my competence, plus an unbiased evaluation by another organization. Accordingly, I sought employment in a highly competitive business, and gave as references three senior officers with whom I had served in the Pentagon. All three gave me strong endorsements, and two weeks later I was employed by a large advertising agency as its Acting Director of Public Relations—at $3,000 a year more than I received as a GS-16 Special Assistant to Secretary Wells. Within six weeks I was writing speeches for the president of the company, who is a very hard man to please. One month later I was promoted, over the heads of other staff members who had been there for years, to Director of Public Relations—an exacting assignment with heavy responsibilities requiring the exercise of considerable tact and judgment—obviously beyond the capabilities of any individual whose mentality was even slightly unbalanced.

"I have now fulfilled my part of our understanding: I testified before your committee, informed my superiors as you directed, and accepted the consequences—loss of position, career, friends, and having to start all over at the age of 46. I have also voluntarily submitted to a psychiatric examination, as you asked me to do. I even went further, and exposed myself to possible financial disaster by asking Secretary Wells for an endorsement which I knew would either make or break my case and my ability to make a living.

"You are probably wondering why, after the setbacks I suffered, I now risk a new career and expose myself to a possible repetition of the worst ordeal I ever experienced. Let me assure you that it's not pride, nor stubbornness, nor rancor; with a wonderful wife and three fine young children depending on me, I'd be idiotic to indulge any personal feelings. I'm set for life here, and I don't want anything to ruin a wonderful setup that I fought so hard to get—under circumstances anything but ideal.

"The answer is simply that I cannot forget the oath of office I took when I first put on a uniform which I wore with pride for more than twenty years. The Defense Department is still being undermined by its own people, on active duty and in uniform. Specific anti-morale activities which I reported in my sworn testimony before your committee have continued without hindrance. Official government publications are still openly endorsing books, films, and magazines which are injurious to the prestige of our men in uniform and our will to resist. This has been going on ever since I first reported it to the GBS, under the mistaken impression that they could do something about it.

"The only hope I can see, if we are to survive as a nation, is to let the public know what is going on and what we face if it is continued at the present rate—and I sincerely believe that your committee has done more to alert the public than any single group. As your committee recently disclosed, a prominent American reporter confessed that he was sent as a Soviet spy to Finland to find out only one thing—the extent of the will to resist. And that is what we're up against here—an all-out attack on our morale and our will to fight, aimed at the nation's youth and its armed forces.

"If I can assist in any way to help you make a case against those who are responsible for permitting this situation to develop and those who are still actively assisting the enemy's efforts to sabotage our military defenses, please let me know. Sincerely yours."

Brett laid down the letter and looked at Jane. Her eyes were brimming, but she smiled through her tears as she said in a choked voice, "Sign it, darling! Oh, you *must* sign it! And mail it tonight!"

CHAPTER TWENTY-FIVE

End of the Panderers

The next morning Brett's letter was delivered to the office of Paul Jardine, who had left only a week before for a three-months' investigation of Communist-inspired riots against American troops stationed in Japan. The letter was opened by a young lawyer who had just been assigned to the office as an administrative assistant during Jardine's absence. He sent for the file containing Brett's testimony. Attached to the file was a card signed by Senator Gunther and addressed to his successor, the new Chairman of the Senate Committee on National Security: "Notice! This case involves highly controversial testimony by a witness whose mental competence has been challenged by the Surgeon General. Before re-opening this case, be sure to check first with Paul Jardine, who knows all the complications."

The administrative assistant handed Brett's letter and the file back to Jardine's secretary. "Add this letter to the file," he said, "and put it back with a notation that this case is not to be re-opened until Mr. Jardine returns. It's the last case I'd want to tackle just now, with those Supreme Court decisions hanging over our heads. We'll be lucky if they don't put us out of business before Congress returns."

"Shall I acknowledge the letter?" Jardine's secretary asked.

"No, I don't think so. If this fellow's really a crack-pot, we'd be sticking our necks out. Remember that psychopath who flim-flammed one of the Washington newspapers into paying him several thousand dollars for his imaginary testimony about Senator O'Hara? This might well be a similar case. If we answer the letter, or even acknowledge it, we'd be on record as having encouraged this fellow. I'll notify the Chairman and make sure that no letter goes out from his office."

Brett waited a month before he told Jane that his letter had never been answered or acknowledged. "I'm not surprised, under the circumstances," he said. "The Supreme Court has been murdering the Congressional investigating committees. Even the Government Bureau of Security was virtually crippled by Supreme Court decisions, until the Director took his case to the people and Congress passed a special bill to protect the GBS files from being thrown open for inspection by enemy agents. And no one can be prosecuted for advocating the overthrow of the U.S. Government unless he first specifies what he's going to do and then actually tries to do it."

Jane was horrified. "Brett, are we completely helpless? Are we just going to sit here and let the enemy take over this country without a fight?"

"Not by a long shot," Brett replied emphatically. "We still haven't used our greatest weapon—an aroused public opinion, backed by the power of the press. The public is already concerned about the way we're drifting. They suspect something's wrong, but they're not sure just what it is or who's to blame. A few patriotic organizations are trying to alert the rest of the country, but they're scattering their shots against half a dozen secondary targets instead of co-ordinating their efforts and concentrating on the real enemy—the Communist agents and fellow-travelers in this country who are helping the Kremlin to weaken us for the kill."

"But how can the public be alerted, when even Congress is unable to protect itself?"

"The Soviets themselves will do it. They can't resist over-playing their hand. Almost any day now, they'll announce something spectacular with the idea of scaring us into submission. They'll announce it on a weekend, hoping to catch us napping like the Japs did when they launched the Pearl Harbor attack early on a Sunday morning. It'll probably be a demonstration of some kind of new super-weapon with implications of atomic capabilities, and they'll use it as a form of diplomatic blackmail with military overtones, in order to frighten our allies into denying us the use of our overseas military bases. But it will backfire on them and have just the opposite effect. The free nations will close ranks and the people of this country will forget their differences and unite just as they did after Pearl Harbor."

"Will there be another war?"

"There's war right now—shooting war—in scattered areas all around the world. But I don't believe the Soviets will risk a big war, for fear their own slaves will turn on them. They still hope we'll have a depression, or spend ourselves into bankruptcy, or commit suicide by negotiating with them on their terms. They're banking heavily on a combination of economic and psychological warfare to beat us without a fight. That's why they make all their major propaganda announcements on weekends, hoping to drive the stock market down and start a financial panic. Thirty years ago that might have done the trick, but not today. But they'll keep trying, until they make some foolish mistake that will offend all civilized nations—just like they did in Hungary."

"But nobody did anything to stop them from crushing the Hungarian revolt. Why will it be any different now?" Jane asked.

"Because they've misjudged the temper of the American people. They think we're too soft, and that we won't fight. Hitler and Tojo made the same mistake, and so did the last German Kaiser. We're a peace-loving nation, but we've never let anyone shove us around. Those who've mistaken our tolerance for timidity have always been rudely surprised. Now the Soviets are making the same mistake, and they've already gone too far. Just take a look at this magazine."

Brett handed Jane a copy of one of the so-called men's magazines. On the front cover was a full-color picture of the President of the United States, and the lead article carried the President's by-line.

"Go ahead," Brett said. "Turn the pages."

Jane gasped as she saw articles which described the superiority of Communist planes and pilots, which depicted American officers as cowards, murderers and mutineers, and which were illustrated with official Department of Defense photographs showing American ships being sunk and U.S. soldiers being slaughtered. Another feature described how an enlisted man got rich during the war by operating a house of prostitution which was patronized by U.S. Counter-intelligence officers and by the Colonel in command of the division.

"It's simply unbelievable!" Jane said. "How can they

dare to print anything like that, right in the same magazine with an article by the President?"

"They think we're simpletons who don't care, and they're flaunting their ability to ridicule us and make fools of us. Copies of that magazine are probably being passed around the Kremlin right now, to show what dolts we are and how helpless we are to prevent even our own magazines from using the prestige of our Commander-in-Chief to undermine the morale of his own troops."

"But surely the President didn't authorize this, Brett!"

"What's the difference? The effect is just the same, and no one's doing anything to stop it. That article was published more than four months ago, and the magazine's still publishing the same kind of material. If our law enforcement agencies were on their toes, the publishers of that magazine would be behind bars right now."

"Are our courts completely helpless?"

"Under our present laws, yes. Over a year ago I collected more than fifty different magazines which are doing this sort of thing. I bought them right in the Pentagon itself, and I submitted them with official U.S. government publications which openly endorsed them—*documented, provable evidence of subversive activities endorsed by senior U.S. officers on active duty and in uniform*. And you know what happened: the same magazines are still going strong, and I was nearly locked up in a mental ward. But this time it's going to be different."

"How, Brett? The Committee won't even answer your letter. What can you do—one man alone, against this kind of opposition?"

"A year ago I was helpless, because the public was complacent about our military superiority and apathetic about the threat of Communist subversion. But that attitude changed fast, after we learned that the Soviets were far ahead of us in the development of intercontinental missiles. Some of our civic groups even got concerned about some of the more obviously objectionable magazines—on moral grounds. One of our biggest associations of women's clubs started a nationwide drive to eliminate these panderers, and the Director of the GBS came out strongly against pornographic magazines, which he called a national menace."

"Yes, I remember that big scandal trial about all the movie stars who were smeared by some smutty magazine. But nothing came of that, as I recall. Didn't the publishers win the case?"

"No, it ended with a hung jury and the judge declared it a mistrial, after the jury wrangled over the case for nearly two weeks. One juror was shunned by the others, who said that he'd been bribed to hold out for acquittal. Furthermore, it was an easy case to beat, because it was tried in a *State* court, where the magazines were charged with violating the State obscenity laws—which are full of loopholes. The defense submitted more than a hundred books and several hundred magazines filled with material just as objectionable, and the jury was hopelessly confused."

"Wouldn't they use the same defense again?"

"Not if it's tried in a Federal court," Brett said. "They tried the wrong people, in the wrong court, on the wrong charges. What the American people don't understand is that this is no longer a question of *morals* but of *national security,* involving our survival as a nation. These magazines should be charged not merely with violating the anti-obscenity laws of our various States, but with subversive activities against the U.S. Armed Forces—which is a *Federal* offense."

"Yes, Brett, but how long will it be before the Federal government wakes up?"

"About a week," Brett said. "Just a few days from now, one of the country's biggest newspapers will publish a series of articles that will jolt the Pentagon from top to bottom. I helped write this series, after I recalled how Dr. Hugo Nilsson told me that one man alone can't clean out Washington's Augean Stables. But he forgot his Greek mythology: one man did clean out the original Augean Stables. Remember how Hercules did the job? He simply diverted a river through the place—a flood of water which washed the stables clean. And that's the way to do the job today—by turning on a flood of public indignation that will flush out all the panderers and purveyors of filth."

Brett held up the magazine with the President's picture on the cover. "A copy of this magazine will be sent to the White House for comment before the story is released. But a picture of the magazine article will be published, showing the President's by-line featured in a magazine filled with smut, and I don't think he'll take that lying down. And one of the articles will cover a scurrilous article attacking our women in uniform, charging that they were and are nothing but paid prostitutes, working in shifts in barracks brothels from which enlisted men are excluded—but where officers, Congressmen, and VIP's receive preferential treatment."

Jane's face lighted up. "Oh, boy! Wait until Congress sees that one! They'll be madder than hornets!"

"That's nothing compared with how mad the wives and mothers of servicemen will get when they see their husbands and sons pictured as poor slobs, cowards and suckers who are led by officers who are blundering fools.

There are fifty million U.S. women over twenty-one, and once they learn what's going on, the fur will really fly."

"Do you think one newspaper can give this story enough circulation?"

"No, but when the women's clubs, the PTA's, and the veterans' organizations swing into action, their combined moral force will sweep the country like an irresistible flood. Reprints of these articles will be made available to them at cost. And this series covers only one phase of the whole sorry situation. Wait until the public hears the rest of the story—about the tie-in between the books, the movies, the family magazines, and the anti-morale operators in the Pentagon. For months I've been working on a book—after hours at the office, at night and on weekends, and it's now at the printer's. It'll be out in a couple of months—right after Congress gets back—and it tells the whole story. One of the big press associations will syndicate it from coast to coast, and it'll also be filmed for the television networks."

"Brett! Why didn't you tell me?"

"I had to work out all the distribution details first. I discussed it with Max Escotti, who was pessimistic at first. He told me that even if I could get it published—which he doubted very much—I'd never get it sold or displayed in the book stores. But there's more than one way to skin a cat. There are only three thousand book stores in this country, but there are six million members of veterans' organizations and eleven million women's clubs members, and they're all interested in fighting subversion. Two big mail-order houses have offered to distribute the book at a special discount, so we don't need the book stores."

"It all sounds wonderful, Brett, except for one thing:

you're bound to be attacked by all the left-wingers and pinkoes, who'll do their best to smear you."

"I've already thought of that, and I'd be willing to accept it for myself, but I've got to protect you and the children. So I'm using a pen-name—one that'll be recognized instantly in the Pentagon. It's an old three-letter signal we used during one of the biggest aerial battles of the war—V J F. In voice code it's pronounced *Victor Jig Fox.*"

"What does it mean, Brett?"

"It means *Enemy sighted. Am attacking at once.*"

"I like that. What will you call the book—something just as appropriate?"

"I think so. The name of the book will be *The Pentagon Case,* by 'Colonel Victor J. Fox.' And the first copy will go to the Senate Committee on National Security. By that time I hope they'll be back in business, because fifty million American women will soon be going on the war-path against subversive magazines, books, and movies. And when they do, that will be the beginning of the end of the panderers."

"But won't there be a great outcry against censorship?" asked Jane.

"Censorship isn't even involved. The women's clubs have already shown the way to eliminate obscene magazines. They simply check what is being sold on their neighborhood newsstands and if they see anything salacious they frankly say so to the dealer—who often agrees and removes the magazines from display. If he doesn't, an official protest is made by the women's club or their PTA or their church group, or through a local business, professional, fraternal, or veterans' organization. Once this is done, the retailer quickly sees the light. If he wants to stay in business, he's got to keep his customers. He can't survive a boycott, and nothing stops the sale of obscene magazines faster than unsold merchandise."

"I see. A sort of customer strike."

"Exactly. And it can be extended to books, movies, TV programs, actors, writers, or directors—anything or anyone who produces, circulates or exhibits subversive material in any form—particularly under the guise of entertainment."

"But how will the public know which magazines, books, or programs are subversive?"

"The public isn't dumb," Brett said. "That's why so many movie theaters have closed, and why so many of our so-called comedians have lost their TV sponsors. All the public needs is a little guidance—just as it now gets from the Decency League in the case of immoral movies. There are plenty of patriotic organizations which could start the ball rolling, once they learn what's going on."

"You mean they'd publish a blacklist of subversive material?"

"No. Both of those terms are 'controversial.' You can't *blacklist* a movie, or say it's *subversive*. But if you can give it a 'decency rating'—which is already being done—there's no reason why you can't give it a *patriotic* rating. In time of war, anything which is anti-military is unpatriotic, and pacifists are mighty unpopular in this country when we're at war."

"Then *that's* what this country has got to understand—that we're *already* at war, in a battle for our minds—right here in our own homes and schools."

"That's right," Brett said slowly, "and we're fighting with our backs to the wall."

Epilogue

The foregoing is fiction. The following excerpts from two public addresses by American leaders cover factual situations.

. . . International communism has demonstrated repeatedly that its leaders are quite willing to launch aggression by violence upon the territory and people of other countries. They are even more ready to expand by propaganda and subversion, economic penetration and exploitation, or by a combination of all three methods.

The free world must be alert to all. . . .

Common sense demands that we put first things first.

The first of all firsts is our nation's security. . . . We cannot obtain and retain the necessary level of technical proficiency unless officers and men, in sufficient numbers, will make the armed services their careers. . . . The biggest part of the task is in the hands of you, as citizens. . . . No matter how good your school is—and we have many excellent ones—I wish that every school board and every P. T. A. would this week and this year make one single project their special order of business: to scrutinize your school's curriculum and standards to see whether they meet the stern demands of the era we are entering. . . . Our defense effort, large as it is, goes only far enough to deter and defeat attack. . . .

We will never be an aggressor. We want adequate security. We want no more than adequacy. We will accept nothing less.

—Dwight D. Eisenhower
November 14, 1957

. . . We must not forget that in gaining domination over a billion people in forty years the Communists have relied primarily not on traditional military aggression across national borders, but on other methods. . . . A modern concept of sound industrial public relations is to inform the people properly of the activities of a company. It is just as simple and equally as sound a concept that the United States, which does much that is good, should tell its story to the peoples of the world. This is particularly important when our competitors, the Communists, are spending an estimated five times as much each year as we are in the propaganda and information field. . . . The strongest military establishment in the world will not save our freedom if we fail to meet the threat which the Communists present in the non-military areas . . . our total danger is great. We are in the midst of a world conflict in which the Sputniks are but a single episode. Call it a cold war; or a contest for men's minds; or a race for outer space.

Call it whatever you will. It is, as Mr. Khrushchev has bluntly told us, a war of many phases—military, political, economic, psychological. A total war, calling for all our resoluteness, determination, patriotism, and faith.

—Richard M. Nixon
December 6, 1957